* * *

ADVENTURES OF

AN OLD

MAGGOT

By

Tony Wallis

Copyright © Tony Wallis 2017

Cover design by totld.com.au

ISBN: 978-0-6485226-0-7

www.boomereview.com

tonyw@boomereview.com

Aussie Slang Dictionary
'Maggot'
Noun: A reprehensible or despicable person

TABLE OF CONTENT

PROLOGUE

'Shed door's fixed, it took me ages to get the old hinge off. What about some lunch?'

He walked into the sitting room.

'Look at you, falling asleep and it's only twelve o'clock'.

He put his hand on her shoulder and gave her a gentle shake. When he removed his hand, she slumped over the side of the armchair.

'Jessie!'

'Jessie, what's happening? What's going on?'

******

CHAPTER 1

Grindal Falcon glanced through the window of the taxicab as it pulled away from the cemetery. Two or three people still hovered around the graveside where he had just buried his wife. One of them was his daughter Clare. They had not spoken.

Having few emotional links with the people at the funeral, he had booked the taxi for as long as it would take to get the funeral over with and get back home. The driver did not speak as they sped through the suburban streets on the return journey. The crackle of the two-way radio was muted. Even cab drivers know that grief must be suffered in silence. Grindal suspected the young driver was eager to discard the dour old man in the back seat. *Depression is contagious, death is for old people,* he mused silently.

He stared aimlessly through the cab window as they stopped at a traffic signal. People in shops, people riding bicycles, for them nothing had changed. Life was the same as it had been yesterday and the day before. For him it was different. It was changed forever. Jessie was dead.

When they reached his house, Grindal handed the driver a twenty dollar note and waited for his change. The young man pushed it into his hand and turned quickly, avoiding eye contact.

As the cab sped away, he heard the loud blare of pop music as the young driver cleansed the silence and depression from inside the vehicle.

Grindal walked into the house and closed the door behind him. The stillness surrounded him like an unseen assailant it was thick and almost palpable. He forced himself to face it, refusing to strike it down with the sound of radio or television. And yet he knew that this game he played with himself was merely a diversion to mask his grief.

Sitting in his favourite armchair, he stared across the room at the chair opposite. It was empty. It was finished. Jessie was dead and gone. He must now pull himself together and get on with whatever life offered him.

The following morning, he went into his wardrobe for a clean shirt. There were none left. His clean underwear had run out two days ago. The laundry basket was overflowing with soiled clothing.

The washing machine made a vibrating sound when he eventually found the 'on' switch. There was an array of instructions each highlighting some special function. His hand trembled slightly as he contemplated the choices on display. He pressed the button under the 'large wash' indicator and sighed with relief as water gushed into the bowl. Feeling more confident, he quickly added a cup-full of the blue liquid he had seen Jessie use. Then for good measure, added another half cup. When he returned half an hour later to see how his washing was going, he discovered the laundry almost knee high in soapsuds.

'Shit.'

He scrambled around on his hands and knees until he found the drain in the floor where the suds were coming from. Quickly he blocked it with a folded towel weighed down with a bucket of water.

The fact that he had been forced into the role of housekeeper without warning was no consolation to him. He was a man and came from an era where women did the things around the house. Failing miserably at what he had once thought of as minor domestic chores, reminded him of his inadequacy.

His attempt at ironing was almost as disastrous. He melted a printed windcheater and covered the iron with a sticky substance that refused to clean off.

The main meal of the day usually consisted of vegetables peeled, then placed into a saucepan, boiled for fifteen minutes and then thrown onto a plate with a slice of corned beef. Covering the concoction in tomato sauce enhanced the taste. His attempt to cook meat usually ended in a smoke-filled kitchen.

In the two weeks since the funeral he had spoken only to the man who ran the local delicatessen. The phone had rung a few times, but he had not bothered to answer it.

And so the days passed. He hardly noticed the automated routine that began to fill his empty life. Each day, moving from bedroom to kitchen to sitting room, from radio to television and back to radio, yet not really seeing, not really listening.

His grief climaxed at the beginning of the third week. Grindal absent-mindedly knocked a pan of boiling milk off the stove. As he reached out to catch the falling pan, the hot liquid covered his hands. He let out a long loud cry. It was filled with all the pain, anguish and frustration that he had successfully blocked out since the death of his wife.

He sat down at the kitchen table covering his face with scolded hands. The first few tears he tried to hold back but then; the unresolved grief he had contained for so long forced its way into the open.

Fifteen minutes passed before he finally blew his nose and took a deep breath. He walked slowly to the bathroom. As he leaned over to run cold water over his hands, he barely recognised the reflection that caught him by surprise in the mirror above the basin.

Three weeks ago, he was self-assured, confident, master of his own destiny. Now he was just a useless old prick who couldn't even boil an egg. Everything he touched ended in disaster. That evening Grindal sat in his armchair fondling a small gilt framed picture of Jessie and himself.

He looked across the room at the empty chair opposite.

'I'm not coping very well am I, Jessie,' he said out loud.

The insensitive beat of the wall clock filled the silent void in his head.

******

'What about the lean piece on the tray?' Grindal Falcon challenged the butcher as he watched him throw a fatty piece of meat onto the scales.

'Would you like me to trim the fat off?' replied the red-faced butcher.

'If you did that, there'd be nothing left, just give me the piece on the tray.'

'Like I said, that's for display, just let me trim the f....'

'Look,' interrupted Grindal. 'If you don't want to give me the piece on the tray, just say so, don't fuck around trying to sell me your rubbish.'

'You're always complaining,' said the now irate butcher. 'And don't use that foul language in my shop.' He looked furtively around the shop; there were four other customers all staring intently. 'In fact, why don't you buy your meat from someone else?' he added more confidently.

'Don't worry, I will,' shouted Grindal. 'It's probably dog meat anyway!'

The four customers rolled their eyes in mutual disgust.

'I'll get security onto you if you come in here again,' he heard the butcher shout as the door closed behind him.

Grindal had now been potentially barred from every butcher's shop in the centre. He could still buy meat from the Supermarket, but even there he was not the most cherished customer.

He went there anyway, to buy a frozen chicken. His current experiments of cooking meat in the oven were proving more successful. He removed the meat every fifteen minutes and tested whether it was edible. The chicken was on sale at half price. He looked at it suspiciously, wondering why.

The manager, whom he had confronted several times before regarding the quality of what was supposed to be fresh food, eyed him carefully as he paid for his purchase. Grindal returned the stare in a silent act of defiance.

He left the shopping centre and walked slowly through the dimly lit concrete car park towards the bus stop on the far side. It was quiet, apart from the sound of his own footsteps and the rustle of the plastic bag in his hand. Grindal hated shopping centres, the stuffy air and the shallow glitz of the shop fronts repulsed him and yet he was drawn there at least once each week to re-join humanity, just for a short time. Even though no one spoke to him except the shop assistants, it gave him the feeling of being part of a group, something he needed, yet could not find anywhere else in his present circumstances.

As he negotiated his way through the maze of parked vehicles, a sudden movement off to the right caught his attention. Three youths were huddled around a parked vehicle. They seemed to be excited and were talking to each other in loud whispers.

Grindal moved closer and quietly observed them. They were pushing what appeared to be a long metal hook between the car door and the window. The shortest of the three youths seemed very agitated.

'For fuck sake hurry up Joe,' he said, pushing the other youth against the car door.

'Who are you pushing?'

9

The other youth turned around sharply. As he did so, his eyes fell directly on Grindal, who was still watching intently, some twenty feet away.

'What's your problem grandad?' he shouted.

Grindal turned and attempted to walk away but before he had taken more than a few paces the shorter youth ran across and stood before him. They stared at each other for a few seconds; Grindal cautious and hesitant, the younger man dominant and aggressive.

'Piss off, you old maggot,' growled the youth, accentuating each word.

Grindal's hand clutched tightly around the plastic bag that hung at his side, it contained the frozen chicken. *One good whack ... soon sort this bastard out,* he thought.

The youth glared at him without blinking, a split - second passed. Grindal recognised the cruel glaze that glinted in the staring eyes.

He knew from past experience; he was in a potentially dangerous situation.

'Okay son, sorry son.'

Grindal turned hurriedly and started to walk back towards the shopping centre. He heard the light footfalls behind him and steeled himself for the anticipated blow.

The kick up the backside sent him staggering forward,

falling across the bonnet of a parked car. The frozen chicken fell to the ground rolling some ten metres before it stopped. The youth strolled away laughing and re-joined his companions.

Grindal did not turn around. 'Fuck them,' he said out loud. As the rush of anger took hold of him, he quickly retrieved the frozen chicken and hurled it with all his strength at the retreating youth. It fell harmlessly far short of its target. The three youths decided to beat a hasty retreat and ran off whooping and laughing as they disappeared out of site.

Grindal's anger and frustration eventually subsided. He had long ago come to terms with the fact that weakness and vulnerability formed an inevitable partnership with old age.

******

The journey back home seemed to take longer than usual. Grindal was feeling all of his sixty-seven years. The encounter with the three youths had upset him more than he cared to admit. His fatigue and frustration accentuated the depression and sadness that still lingered in his conscious thoughts.

'Jessie, Jessie, where will it all end,' he sighed under

his breath.

A vision of his late wife flashed across his mind. For some time, he had been talking to her in his head, the habit was becoming frequent. Grindal was aware of this new tendency but he had no friends, no God and everyone needed someone to talk to.

Like most lonely people, he had lots of imaginary conversations. These took place between people he had met, and some he had not. Most of the time the people and situations he disliked most filled these conversations, his glib retorts to questions that would never be asked gave him some comfort.

When he entered the house and closed the front door, the silence enshrouded him like a thick blanket. He immediately turned on the radio. Too much quietness made him despondent, a personal weakness to be avoided. He placed the now battered frozen chicken in the fridge and thought about having something to eat. Standing in front of the open refrigerator, he surveyed the contents. Nothing took his fancy, probably because he wasn't hungry anyway.

Still feeling weary after the trip from the shopping centre Grindal sat in his favourite chair and closed his eyes for what seemed only a moment. He awakened to the sound of the radio playing "Mona Lisa," it used to be Jessie's favourite song. Grindal listened to the melody. A montage of memories danced fleetingly across his mind. He slowly opened his eyes. The room was dark and for an instant he was confused. When he turned on the light Grindal saw from the living room clock that it was eight thirty, he had been asleep for three hours. It didn't really matter. He wasn't going anywhere.

Having not eaten since mid-day, grumbling sounds from his empty stomach reminded him of his hunger. It was too late for a large meal and in any case, he couldn't be bothered. Still feeling tired; he decided tea and toast would do until morning. He put the bread into the toaster and sat back in his chair. On the coffee table that stood next to the chair was a small gilt framed photograph of Jessie and himself. It was his favourite. Next to it was a small hand painted wooden box. He had taken it from a draw in the dressing table that morning but had not yet opened it. It belonged to Jessie. She called it her memory bank. He reached across and carefully lifted the lid from the box.

It contained small keepsakes that had been gathered over the many years they had been together. There were ticket stubs to various shows they had seen, invitations to weddings, special letters and photographs and a silver charm bracelet. The charm bracelet held great significance for

Grindal. For the past ten years it had been a tradition that he would give Jessie one extra charm each year on the day of their anniversary. She never wore the bracelet, preferring to keep it in her special memory bank. Grindal closed his eyes as his mind drifted back to memories of happier times.

******

There was sound of breaking glass and someone shouting.

'Is anyone there?'

Grindal opened his eyes slowly as a favourite memory disappeared from his mind's eye. The room before him was bright yet at the same time his vision was clouded. He was confused. The confusion vanished in a moment as the reality of his situation took hold. The kitchen was no longer visible; it was hidden behind a wall of raging flames. Clouds of grey black smoke surrounded him like angry ghosts. Within seconds he was gasping for air. As he pushed himself from the chair, his eyes fell upon Jessie's memory bank that lay open where he had left it.

Grindal was suddenly filled with panic. The thought of losing this treasured link with the past caused him to cry out in anguish.

In his eagerness to reach it, he stumbled into the table

and tipped it onto its side. The contents of the box along with the photograph were spilled onto the floor. In his momentum Grindal fell full length over the table and landed face down. Clutching hands reached out in desperation, searching for the treasured symbols of his past. He now coughed continuously as his lungs searched desperately for air. He frantically searched for the charm bracelet, but his eyes were so full of smoke he could only grope around in a last vain hope that he might stumble across it.

The heat was now scorching the unprotected skin of his face and hands. The flames had moved quickly from the kitchen and were beginning to devour the surrounding area. The instinct of self-preservation caused Grindal to lift himself from the floor to try and escape the hot fingers of flame that were reaching out to consume him. His head was spinning. He staggered two paces before losing his balance and falling back to the floor. As his hands stretched out before him his fingers felt the shape of a familiar object. It was the small gilt framed photograph. He clutched it tightly pulling it to his bosom. The few last gasps of air in his lungs were sucked out as he dry-reached uncontrollably. His strength was gone he was done for.

Suddenly, a large pair of hands grabbed him roughly under the armpits and began to drag him swiftly across the room. Grindal was almost unconscious. The strong hands that were pulling him towards the door almost lifted him off the ground. Within seconds he was outside the burning house, away from the heat and smoke. His aching lungs automatically sucked in the cold night air. He found himself lying on the grass verge near the roadside. His knees bent double as he tried to clear the acrid smoke from his lungs. Someone pushed a plastic mask onto his face. Without being told, Grindal sucked hungrily at the oxygen that came from it. After a few desperate gulps he was forced to remove the mask, unable to control the need to cough up the smoke from his lungs.

'That's right cough it all up,' said a nearby voice.

The high-pitched noise of a wailing siren drowned out his attempt to reply. Grindal raised himself onto his knees. His head was now beginning to clear. He looked at the burning house. His mind refused to acknowledge the site before him. It was surreal. The flames leapt into the night sky like bright jagged fingers of light pointing upwards and outwards. Sparks of burning debris flew off the blaze like a cascade of fireflies, quickly disappearing as they were picked up by the evening breeze.

As full consciousness dawned on him, Grindal realised the enormity of the situation. His house, his life, his links with the past were almost destroyed. Soon there would be nothing left. When he looked again, five or six fire hoses were bombarding the building. There were shouts and screams as firemen communicated with each other. People were running everywhere. The whole roadway outside the house was filled with a sea of flashing lights.

Someone grabbed him under his armpits and lifted him to his feet.

'Come on old timer, you'll be all right, just take it easy.'

He wiped the tears that were still streaming from his smoke-filled eyes. Something cut into his forehead. It was then he realised he was still clutching the small gilt framed photograph of Jessie and himself. Momentarily embarrassed, he slipped it quickly into his pocket.

His head was now clear. The anguish and frustration he had experienced for the past few minutes was now being quickly replaced by a burning anger. He was filled with a need to hit back. And yet whom could he blame. Who could he vent his anger on?

'What the fuck's going on?' he shouted at the ambulance officer.

'Calm down, calm down,' said the ambulance officer placing his arm around Grindal's shoulder. 'You don't look too good. Let's get you on the stretcher, then we can take you to the hospital for a check-up.'

Grindal pushed him away. 'What do you mean, calm down, that's my fucking house going up in flames. That's everything I own.'

He stared incredulously at the burning shell. The house was a symbol of his independence and security. Something he owned that might link the past to his future. Now it was gone. The enormity of the situation fell upon him like a blackness that cut him to the bone. He could not take his eyes from the fire and watched for what seemed like hours, but was actually only a few minutes, as the flames were brought under control. What was left was a smouldering shell.

The anger and frustration welled up inside of him but there was nothing he could do. Nothing could change what had happened. He looked up to the night sky and let out a cry of grief. He was totally defeated. His emotions quickly drained away until soon there was nothing left, only emptiness.

He allowed the two ambulance men to help him onto the stretcher. There were crowds of people now gathered in the street, all staring and pointing like spectators at a fireworks display. He recognised the faces of many. Some he had known for years, at least by site, neighbours he would nod to occasionally. Yet none tried to communicate with him, they just gazed in silence. The grief in his countenance was unapproachable.

As he was lifted into the ambulance, his jacket caught momentarily on the door. The framed photograph in his pocket fell un-noticed to the ground. As the doors closed, he was immediately cocooned in an eerie silence that insulated him from the bustle and noise outside. Unexpectedly a finger of fear suddenly touched him. He closed his eyes tightly.

'What now Jessie, what happens now?' he whispered.

******

CHAPTER 2

When he awoke the following morning Grindal looked around cautiously. It was daytime; he was lying in a single bed covered with clean crisp white sheets. His memory of the previous night was fragmented. He remembered the fire vividly, but what happened after that was not so clear. He knew he was lying in a hospital bed, but there were curtains drawn tightly around the bed obscuring his vision. There was an oxygen tube clipped to his nose and the right side of his body felt sore. His throat was raw; when he swallowed Grindal could still taste the smoke. He breathed deeply stretching his lungs. The effort made him cough uncontrollably.

A concerned looking nurse swept open the curtains that surrounded his bed.

'Are you alright Mr. Falcon?' she asked anxiously.

Grindal stared at her and said nothing.

'Are you alright?' she repeated.

'What do you think,' he replied sourly.

'You were a bit upset when they brought you in last night; the night sister said they had to give you a very strong sedative.'

'Is that why I can't think straight?'

'Never mind, you'll be all right in a couple of hours.'

Grindal pushed himself up on one elbow and made as if to get out of bed.

'Now just you stay where you are while I check you out.'

The sincere smile she gave him made Grindal feel less irritated. He lay back on the pillow as she busied herself checking his blood pressure and temperature. When she pulled down the bed sheet, he could see why the right side of his body felt so sore. From his rib cage all the way down to his foot was bright red. He winced as she lightly touched his leg with the tip of her finger.

'Sorry,' she said, almost in a whisper as she pulled the sheet back carefully,

'Is there anyone you'd like to get in touch with, any family?'

'No' said Grindal firmly.

She looked at him for a moment. 'The police will probably want to talk to you about the fire. They rang earlier and asked if you were well enough to be interviewed.'

'What, do they think I burned my own house down on purpose'

'No, nothing like that I'm sure, but they do have to make a report. Would you like me to draw the curtain back?'

she said, in an overly cheerful voice.

Grindal did not reply.

'Breakfast will be here soon.'

She turned her back on him and strode away, giving the curtain a well-practiced flick that opened the enclosed space.

The ward was small, four beds on each side. All were occupied. From what he could see, most were elderly men who gazed vacantly at the walls or ceiling. *This must be the geriatrics ward.* The man opposite nodded slightly in his direction. Grindal nodded back, but that was as far as the communication went.

The events of the night before kept flashing across his mind. He could still see the roaring fire that had engulfed his house. The heat was still burning into his side. Yet, for some reason he still couldn't focus on the seriousness of his situation. He decided the sedative he had been given was to blame. It was all too difficult.

When breakfast arrived, he made his selection from the foods on offer. Although he had not been in a hospital for many years, the taste and smell of the food seemed to be as he had remembered it. A real challenge for even the hungriest patient. He sipped sparingly on a cup of lukewarm coffee made with powdered milk. As he did so, a tall man in a dark suit entered the ward and strode purposefully toward his bed. He wore a pair of thick-lensed glasses and a toothy grin. It was not until he had reached the bedside that Grindal noticed the white dog collar around his neck.

He held out his hand. 'Good morning, I'm Reverend Charlesworth, the hospital chaplain.'

'Good morning Charlie, and goodbye.'

Grindal rolled over on his side turning his back on the smiling clergyman; the fact that it was his scalded side endeared him even less to the unwanted visitor. He had no respect for anyone connected to the church and regarded them as a total waste of time.

'Now I know you must be upset, but there are lots of things we must discuss. I only want to help you.' The chaplain placed his hand on Grindal's shoulder.

'I don't need any help from the likes of you, just go away and leave me alone.' Grindal was beginning to lose his temper.

'Now don't be like that,' insisted the Chaplain.

'Just piss off,' said Grindal sourly.

'Show some respect laddie, diny talk to the Reverend like that.'

A new voice had joined the conversation. Grindal looked across to see where the broad Scots brogue had come from. A bald, red faced, old man was staring at him intently from the bed opposite.

'Mind your own business grandad,' said Grindal staring back at the old man.

'Who are you calling grandad heh; I'll be over there and sort you out if you diny mind yer tongue.'

The old man's face was turning a bright purple colour 'Scotts git,' retorted Grindal.

The reverend Charles Charlesworth seemed to be lost for words as he stared from one man to the other.

'Gentlemen, gentlemen, please calm down' he eventually blurted out.

But it was too late; the old Scotsman was now out of his bed and making his way quickly across the ward.

'Diny talk to me like that, ye bastard,' shouted the old man.

Grindal was taken by surprise with the speed the old Scotsman had sprung out of his bed. At first glance, he looked quite comical dressed in his long white hospital gown. He had no hair and no teeth and was now flailing his arms around like a windmill.

'Nurse, nurse, somebody, anybody', shouted the now very much alarmed Reverend Charlesworth.

Recovering from his momentary daze, Grindal slipped his feet out of the bed and stood up, ready to take on the mad

Scotsman, who was now slavering and making grunting noises. The Reverend Charlesworth stepped in between the two men to try and stop the imminent confrontation.

The moment Grindal got to his feet the blood drained from his head, and he fell back onto the bed. Which was just as well, because the flailing fist of the now totally out of control mad Scotsman just missed the side of his face.

The Reverend Charlesworth was not so lucky as the big roundhouse swing caught him square in the eye. His glasses broke in half. He dropped like a stone, wailing in anguish as he hit the hard-concrete floor with the back of his head.

Grindal stared wide-eyed as the berserk Scotsman who was now shouting obscenities and bearing down on him. He covered his face and closed his eyes waiting for the impending blows. Luckily the blows never came. A very large orderly saved the situation when he grabbed the flailing old man from behind, pinning his arms and lifting him off the ground.

'Let me go, I'll kill the bastard,' shouted the old man.

'Calm down Mr. McDougal, calm down,' said the large orderly, who seemed to have no problem whatsoever in restraining his captive. He lifted him like a rag doll and carried him back to his own bed.

Grindal opened his eyes just in time to see the nurse

inject the mad McDougal with what must have been a very strong sedative.

Within seconds the old man's arms flopped down to his sides, and his head fell forward.

'Silly old bugger,' said the smiling orderly.

The nurse was still not sure exactly what had happened. She walked over to Grindal's bedside.

'Are you alright Mr. Falcon?'

'Don't worry about me I'm fine. He never laid a glove on me.'

Reverend Charlesworth was now back on his feet rubbing his head with one hand and covering his eye with the other. He was groaning softly, 'Oh, my god, my god.'

The nurse was trying her best to comfort him. 'What happened here, Charles, whatever was it that caused Mr. McDougal to go off his head like that?'

'We were just having a chat together when that mad Scotsman charged over and started laying into us,' piped in Grindal.

The Chaplain stared at him blankly for a few moments before the nurse led him away to treat his injuries. Grindal chuckled to himself. 'Sorted out that bastard all right.'

He looked across at the bed opposite. The curtains were drawn tightly. Grindal guessed they must have given the mad Scotsman a very serious dose of something. All he could hear was heavy breathing. The rest of the patients in the ward avoided eye contact with him. When the nurse came back into the ward, she treated him rather coldly, he reasoned that she must have heard the Reverend Charlesworth's version of the fracas. This did not disturb him. He was totally unrepentant and believed the crazy Scotsman and the preacher both got what they deserved.

Later that morning the doctor gave him a thorough examination and informed Grindal he would be well enough to be discharged by Friday. This meant he had two more nights' accommodation, after that he was looking for somewhere to live. The doctor's pronouncement brought home to him the gravity of his situation. Since he had arrived in the hospital, Grindal had avoided thinking of his predicament. Now it was becoming blatantly clear. He would soon have to make some plans for his immediate future.

His first thought was to find out exactly what he had brought into the hospital the previous night. He couldn't recall whether he had taken his wallet out of his back pocket before he fell asleep in the chair. A sudden urgency fell upon him as he recalled the photograph he had slipped into his pocket after he had been dragged from the house. A quick investigation of his bedside draw revealed nothing. Grindal pressed the call button and anxiously waited until the nurse arrived. When she did, he spoke to her quite sharply.

'My stuff, what happened to it?'

'I beg your pardon,' she said defensively.

'My clothes, the stuff I came in with, where is it?'

'If you just wait a minute, I'll find out for you. And don't get cross with me, I'm just the hired help, I didn't put you in here.'

Grindal tried to rein in his anxiety. 'I'm sorry, but I just need to find out what I came in with.'

She turned and left in a huff. Grindal heard a snigger from across the ward. It was the mad McDougal. When he looked across the man stared up at the ceiling, but he was still smiling.

The nurse returned some twenty minutes later carrying some clothes and his wallet, all of which she dumped on the bed apart from the shoes which she put on the floor.

'Please put them in the cupboard when you've finished,'

'What about the photograph?' Grindal said anxiously.

'That's it, that's all there is,' she replied.

'But the photograph, there was a small gilt framed photograph, I'm sure, I put it in my pocket, I know I did.'

The nurse sensed his alarm. 'Look, I'm sure this is everything. I'll double check with Sister, but I'm certain there was no photograph. Just try and calm down, I know you've had a bad experience, but getting angry with the people around you won't solve anything.'

She turned and left him to inspect the small pile of clothing and his wallet. The trousers and shirt were torn and scorched and beyond repair, he consigned them straight to the rubbish bin. He was left with a pair of black shoes, some cream coloured socks, a worn-out singlet and a pair of black underwear. There was no photograph.

Grindal was heartbroken. The photograph was his only tangible link with the past. 'I'm sorry Jessie It's gone. It's all gone,' he mumbled to himself.

Grindal turned his attention to the wallet. It contained thirty dollars in cash, an out of date driving licence and his pension card. Looking at the wallet caused him to think how much he had in his savings account. He was not sure; Jessie had looked after that side of things. Probably a few hundred dollars at most, not much to show for a lifetime on this planet, he thought dejectedly.

Later that afternoon a visit from the police had confirmed his worst fears. The house he and Jessie had lived in for all those years was now a burnt-out shell. An investigation by the fire department concluded that a faulty electrical appliance caused the fire. Grindal grimaced when he thought of the toaster that had been playing up for the past two weeks.

'Never mind,' the Sergeant had said, 'the insurance will pay for all the cleanup.'

'What insurance,' Grindal had replied.

With that, the policeman had shaken his head, wished him good luck and left.

For the rest of that day Grindal had slipped into a state of despair. Sleep that night was impossible. He tossed around in his bed and did not fall asleep until the early hours around in his bed and did not fall asleep until the early hours of the morning.

The following day he was awakened early from his fitful sleep by the noise and activity in the ward. He declined breakfast apart from a cup of the luke-warm coffee he had now learned to tolerate. There was a new nurse on duty; she had a few kind words for him, which for some reason raised his spirits a little.

'Good morning Mr. Falcon, how are you feeling today? Not too much pain I hope?'

Grindal nodded his head in acknowledgement as she

walked swiftly past, heading for the other side of the ward where some old codger was having a coughing fit. He watched as the nurse held the old man erect whilst she patted him firmly on the back. The man's breakfast tray had spilled all over the bed.

I wonder whether he was trying to get it up or get it down, mused Grindal thoughtfully. The mad McDougal stared at him threateningly across the ward. He lowered his gaze, the last thing he wanted that morning was a fistfight.

Around midday the nurse walked over to him smiling.

'Cheer up Mr. Falcon. You've got a visitor.'

Grindal watched warily as the man approached his bedside. He was tall and muscular, probably in his late fifties. The feature that really made him stand out was the huge smile he was wearing.

'I don't want any counseling or any bullshit messages from Jesus,' said Grindal before the man had even spoken.

'Don't worry mate, I'm not a preacher or a counselor,' said the man, still smiling.

'Then who are you?'

'I'm the silly bastard that pulled you out of your house the other night,' replied the man.

Grindal was startled by this announcement and for a moment did not know what to say. His visitor on the other hand was still smiling as he thrust his hand out.

'Roy . . . Roy Thatcher.'

'Grindal Falcon... Pleased to meet you Roy.'

Grindal stared into the big grinning face and wondered what to say next. He was not accustomed to thanking anyone for anything, but in this instance his obligation was obvious.

'Thanks very much for doing what you did Roy, if it wasn't for you, I would have gone up with the house.' The thought jumped into his head that going up with the house might have solved all of his problems.

'Nothing to it,' said the big man. 'So how are you feeling anyway?' he added.

'Not bad, considering . . .'

'Here, I've got something for you,' said Roy. He then reached into his inside pocket and pulled out the small gilt framed photograph of Grindal and Jessie.

'I thought you might be looking for this,' he said, as he handed Grindal the photograph.

'Dam right I was!' said Grindal.

There was a lump in his throat and tears welled up in his eyes.

'Thank you, thank you,' he whispered staring at the photograph.

Roy said nothing preferring to let Grindal enjoy the

moment. A few seconds past before Grindal recovered from the sudden burst of emotion that had taken him by surprise. He took a long sniff through his nose and cleared his throat.

'I hope you didn't get burnt?' offered Grindal.

'No, I'm fine,' said Roy. 'Pity about the house though, I went past there yesterday, I'm afraid it's completely burnt out.'

'Yeah, I know. The police told me.'

'Are you insured?' asked Roy.

'No,' replied Grindal.

'Oh shit... what a bastard... where will you go?'

'Don't worry, I'll find somewhere.'

'Do you have family?' asked Roy.

'No not really, . . . Well I do have a daughter, but we haven't spoken for the last couple of years. A few arguments, you know what I mean?'

'Yes, I know what you mean about family arguments,' laughed Roy.

'Anyway, as I said, I'll find somewhere, don't worry about me,' asserted Grindal.

There was a short period of silence between the two men.

'When do you get out?'

'Tomorrow.'

Roy looked around the ward. 'These places never change, do they?'

'Your right there... How long since you were in a hospital...?'

The two men chatted for quite some time. In the course of the conversation Roy explained that on the night of the fire he had been visiting a friend who had just moved into the same suburb that Grindal had lived in. Being unsure of the exact location Roy had stopped the car to consult his street directory. Luckily, he had stopped right outside Grindal's house. It was then that he had seen the flickering flames through the front window of the house. Having been a member of the Emergency Fire Service in his younger days, he was automatically motivated to take immediate action. It was this coincidence that had probably saved Grindal's life.

As the conversation between the two men continued, neither divulged much information about their personal circumstances. This suited Grindal and in a very short space of time he began to relax. Both were careful not to talk about anything that might seem to intrude on the other's privacy.

Roy was one of those fortunate people who were successful in business early in life. By the time he was fifty he had made enough money to retire. Not in the lap of luxury, but comfortably, as he put it. He shared a house with a friend of his called Damien.

Their conversation was interrupted by the afternoon tea trolley.

'I'd invite you to have a cup of coffee, but I wouldn't want you to throw up on the way home,' said Grindal.

Roy stared down at his wristwatch.

'Shit, look what the time is.'

A few seconds passed in silence with Roy still looking thoughtfully at his watch.

'Look, why don't you come and stay with me for a couple of days, just till you get sorted out?' said Roy, breaking the silence.

Grindal was surprised.

'But you don't even know me. Why should you do that for me? Anyway, I wouldn't want to put you out.'

'Look, the bloke I share my house with won't mind so there's no real problem. You can sleep in the spare room.'

Grindal thought for a while, he had few options and the few hundred dollars he had wouldn't last long staying in a hotel.

'Well, I would really appreciate it, just for a couple of days, just until I find somewhere more permanent.'

'Well that's settled then, would you like me to pick you up?' asked Roy.

'No mate she's right, I'll make my own way there when they let me out.'

Roy took out a piece of paper and wrote down his

address and telephone number. He stood up to leave.

'This is where we live' he said, handing the piece of paper to Grindal

'Well I'll see you some time tomorrow then,' said Grindal.

'That's okay, I'm home all day, just give me a ring and let me know when you're coming. I'll see you later then.'

'Thanks very much', said Grindal feeling awkward.

He relaxed and lay back on his pillow and watched as the big man strode out of the ward. When Roy left, Grindal was feeling much better, he liked the man. For him that was an experience he had not felt for some time. He was impressed with everything about Roy Thatcher. 'Top man,' he mused to himself.

He picked up the photograph that was on the cabinet next to the bed, looked at it for a few seconds, kissed it lightly, and then carefully placed it in the draw with his wallet.

Now at least he had somewhere to go when he left the hospital. As he contemplated his immanent release it suddenly struck him that he had no clothes to wear. *Surely there must be somewhere I can get a few clothes.* He waited until the nurse was passing through the ward.

'Nurse, have you got a minute?' he asked, in a raised

voice. She seemed to be in a big hurry.

'Yes, Mr. Falcon?'

'I was wondering, is there anywhere I can get some clothes? I'll probably be leaving tomorrow, and I've just realized I don't have anything to wear except my underwear and a pair of shoes.'

'No worries,' she said as she started to walk away. 'That's the Chaplain's department. I'll get him to come and see you. Reverend Charlesworth is his name. He'll fix you up.'

With that she was gone and Grindal was left to contemplate what reception he might get from Reverend Charlesworth.

He didn't have long to wait; about an hour later the frowning Reverend approached his bed.

'I hope we're in a better frame of mind today?' he said.

'Yes... Yes, much better thank you,' said Grindal. He had to force himself to make eye contact with the man.

'So, what can I do for you Mr. Falcon? Nurse said something about you needing some clothes.'

'Well yes, I do actually,' said Grindal awkwardly. 'Mine were all destroyed in the fire when my house burnt down. All I need is just a pair of trousers and a shirt or a pullover or something. Anything will do. I can bring them back as soon as I get a chance to buy some.'

The Reverend Charlesworth pursed his lips.

'What size are you?'

'Medium will be fine,' said Grindal hurriedly.

There was a short silence.

'Yes, I'm sure I'll be able to fix you up with something just right,' said the Reverend, with just the hint of a smile.

'Is there anything else?'

'No that's it thanks.'

The reverend shook his head and walked away.

'You can say a little prayer for me if you like,' Grindal shouted after him; and then regretted it. The Reverend Charlesworth did not respond.

******

The following morning, he was feeling much more positive. He ate a large breakfast then read the paper for an hour whilst he waited for the doctor. As soon as he was given the all-clear Grindal was in a hurry to leave. There was no sign of his clothes, so he decided to ask the nurse. She came back five minutes later.

'These must be yours,' she said handing him a brown paper bag with 'Mr. Falcon' written in large print on the front. 'They were in the nurse's station. Reverend Charlesworth must have left them there.'

'Thanks very much,' said Grindal as he took the bag. The nurse left him in a flurry muttering about things to be done.

He emptied the contents onto the bed. 'What the fuck'…. The Reverend Charlesworth had taken his revenge. A red plaid jacket, green shirt and white trousers lay on the bed before him. He stared at them in disbelief; he was normally a most conservative dresser.

'Fuck it, who cares anyway,' he muttered. Grindal dressed himself. The trousers were too short, and the jacket was too large. He was glad there was no mirror.

As he was about to leave the ward, he turned to find the old Scotsman glaring at him. 'You must be goin back to the circus then,' leered McDougal.

Grindal stuck up his middle finger. 'Scotts git,' he shouted. Then turned and left before the old man could launch himself out of bed. He laughed, more so to hide his own nervous tension, rather than finding any mirth in the situation, as he heard the mad McDougal shouting obscenities behind him. He tried to centre his thoughts on the present as the anticipation of leaving the hospital temporarily masked his uncertainty of what might lie ahead.

******

CHAPTER 3

Roy Thatcher lived in the Eastern suburbs. When the taxi that had brought Grindal to the house drove away he was tempted to just walk away and forget the whole idea. The white paling fence and the neatly clipped lawn reminded him of his own house when Jessie had tended the garden. But his wife was now dead and so was the house. He pushed the memories from his consciousness and focused on the present.

Taking a deep breath, he made his decision.

'What the hell.'

He knocked firmly on the front door. His apprehension was relieved somewhat when Roy opened the door. He welcomed Grindal like a long-lost brother.

'Come in mate, come in. How are you feeling?' said Roy, still with the same big smile on his face.

'Bit like a circus clown dressed like this'

Grindal wiped his feet nervously and stepped inside.

'Come and sit down I'll make some coffee.'

'That'll be good. It'll be nice to drink some real coffee for a change.'

Roy fussed around him like a mother hen, which made

Grindal feel embarrassed. They spent the next fifteen minutes talking about nothing in particular. When they had finished their coffee, Roy left the table and headed for the back door.

'Before I forget I'd better introduce you to Eric and his best mate,' he said with a smile.

Grindal was confused. 'I thought you said your friends name was Damien?'

'It is', he replied. Damien will be away until tomorrow evening; he's visiting his mother in Sydney. These are Damien's friends.'

He opened the door and gave a short whistle. Within seconds an excited yapping miniature poodle wobbled into the room, followed by a large grey Siamese cat. The poodle headed straight for Grindal and jumped up, resting its legs on his chair, he then saw the reason for the wobbling gait. Eric only had three and a half legs.

'I hope you don't mind animals?' said Roy.

'No, I don't mind at all,' he lied. 'Did he have an accident or something?' asked Grindal.

'Yes, he's a naughty boy,' said Roy picking the dog up in his arms. 'You don't play near Daddy anymore when he's chopping wood do you?' said Roy as Eric licked him all over the face. 'What a day that was,' he added.

Meanwhile the Siamese had entwined itself around Grindal's leg and he was desperately resisting the temptation to kick it away. He classed cats at the same level as the clergy but realised this was not the time to offer his opinion.

'I see Mr. Dick has taken a fancy to you,' said Roy.

Grindal eyed the cat trying to disguise his contempt. 'That's an unusual name for a cat.'

'Yes, Mr. Dick the Second is his full name, Damien chose it; the cat was a gift from an old friend of his called Richard. He absolutely adores him... Anyway, enough of the menagerie, I'll show you your room'.

Grindal extricated himself from the cat and followed Roy down the hallway to the spare room.

'Make yourself comfortable. I'll be in the kitchen if you want anything.'

Grindal turned to Roy. 'I really appreciate this,' he said. 'Mind you, it's Just for a couple of days, that's all.' Grindal was assuring himself as much as he was his host.

Roy closed the door behind him. Grindal sat on the bed and looked around. The room was clean and looked as if it had been freshly painted. There was a strange looking picture of two naked men hanging on the wall opposite the bed. Grindal was not too impressed by it but reasoned he had no appreciation of art and therefore should not comment.

Apart from the single bed there was a small dressing table, and a built-in wardrobe.

'Can't complain about this. This is really nice.'

******

The following morning Grindal decided he should inspect his own house to see if there was anything worth salvaging. Roy offered to take him in his car but he was determined to go by himself. He knew it might be an emotional experience, something he preferred not to share. He was still repressing the events of the previous weeks. The sense of loss and despair that caused an ache in the pit of his stomach refused to go away.

When they finished breakfast Grindal spent a few minutes studying the public transport timetable.

One hour later he stepped out of the bus at the top of Harris Street. The Street he had lived in for more than thirty years. He walked slowly down the route he had taken a thousand times before. Every house, every telegraph pole was familiar. For reasons he could not fathom, his sense of awareness seemed to be heightened. Even the unkempt gardens took on a strange significance. His eyes roamed everywhere. Not like usual, when they fixed themselves on the pavement, not seeing, not caring what was happening anywhere outside that point of awareness.

The few people who were around took no notice of him. He had never talked much to his neighbors or anyone else in the street for that matter, yet by sight he knew them all. Like himself, they all had a story to tell, but no one was interested in listening.

As Grindal approached the blackened ruin that was once his house, his heart began to pound and his whole body began to shake. The shock hit him much more than he had anticipated. Grabbing what was left of the garden fence he steadied himself. His mind filled with precious memories that flashed before him in quick succession. The day he and Jessie had first seen it. The day they had moved in; his daughter Clare playing in the front garden. And finally, the day after Jessie's funeral when he had sat, alone in the front room in total despair. The shell of the house on the blackened piece of land looked almost surreal. The roof was gone as were the front door and windows.

As he stared at the ruin, a picture flashed into his mind of how it had looked when Jessie had been alive. A small double-fronted cottage with freshly painted windows and gutters enclosed by a bull nosed verandah. The garden had been immaculate. Planted out in traditional country cottage

45

style. People who walked past the house used to stop and admire it. It had been Jessie's pride and joy.

The vision faded quickly. The stark reality of the burnt-out shell brought him back to the present. As the shaking in his legs gradually subsided, he ventured through the gate. There was nothing standing. Everything inside had been destroyed. Blackened debris that was once his furniture formed unrecognisable heaps of ash throughout each room. The kitchen could only be identified by the scorched sink top that hung precariously from the broken waste pipe. There was black sludge in most of the house where water from the fire hoses had not yet dried out.

Grindal pulled and pushed his way through the piles of debris. Frantically searching for something, anything that might partially compensate for the profound sense of loss he felt throughout his whole being. Eventually, his hands and face covered in soot, his clothes filthy, he gave up.

He wandered out into the back yard. The small shed that had once housed his lawnmower and garden tools was empty; the contents probably stolen and already sold to the second-hand shop. Staring at the ruin he battled for long minutes with anger, despair, sadness, and frustration, a mixture of negative emotions that refused to be controlled.

In the end, it was anger that won the conflict. Grindal

was glad it won. It gave him strength to carry on. It was anger that sustained him when Jessie was killed.

'Fuck the house,' he voiced out loud. Then trudged back through the ruin and into the street.

He walked purposefully back to the bus stop staring at the pavement in front of him. As he boarded the bus, the driver stared at him, as did the other passengers. His grimy clothes and blackened face made him look somewhat comical, like a chimney sweep from some bizarre parody. But when they looked into his eyes, they turned away quickly, they had darkness in them that said, keep out of my way, or else....

When he arrived back at Roy's place, Roy was out. Grindal was relieved, he did not feel like talking, and it allowed him to get cleaned up. After taking a shower, he placed all his blackened clothes in the washing machine, and then into the clothes dryer. By the time Roy returned they were clean. A loose sweater he had borrowed from Roy hid his crumpled shirt. The activity had been good for him it allowed him time to bring his emotions under control.

Roy went straight to the fridge, took out two cans of beer and offered one to Grindal. 'How did it go?' he asked.

'Just as I expected,' replied Grindal. 'A big pile of ashes and not much else.'

Roy seemed to sense that Grindal's anger and did not press him too much for details.

'What are you going to do about the mess? If you wait for the council to clean it up, they'll charge you a fortune.'

'Yes, I suppose you're right. Maybe I should look in the yellow pages and get a few prices from some rubbish removal contractors.' Grindal took a long drink from his can.

'Why not wait until tomorrow?' said Roy enthusiastically. 'Damien will be back. He knows this bloke who has a backhoe and a truck, maybe he could give you a good price.'

'That's a start anyway,' agreed Grindal.

He'd forgotten about Damien. He wondered what kind of person he was. But on the basis that Roy was such a good scout, there couldn't be too much wrong with him he reasoned.

'Anyway, just to change the subject. Now your friends coming back, I'll be looking for somewhere more permanent to stay,' said Grindal as he finished off his can of beer.

'Don't worry about that, Damien won't mind. I told him all about you and as far as he's concerned your welcome to stay as long as you like.'

Grindal did not reply, he still could not fathom why a complete stranger would take him in and offer so much for no apparent reason. He knew it was something he would not do himself, a fact that made him feel even more guilty about the whole situation.

After two more cans of beer they decided to eat. Grindal felt uneasy because, as usual, Roy insisted on preparing the meal. He alleviated his guilt somewhat by washing the dishes. They sat and watched television for two hours before Grindal decided to have an early night.

The next day Roy was very chirpy. He seemed to be excited by the fact that Damien was coming home. Grindal could not quite understand why. From lunchtime onwards, Roy kept looking out of the window and glancing at his watch. Grindal cloistered himself in the kitchen and buried his head in the newspaper. He didn't much like meeting new people and Roy's antics were beginning to make him nervous.

A loud blast from his car horn eventually heralded Damien's arrival.

'He's here. He's here,' exclaimed Roy excitedly. 'Let's help him with his stuff.' Roy ran out of the door.

Grindal waited in nervous anticipation. *Something's not quite right here.*

A moment later Roy and Damien came in the door together, arms around each other.

49

Damien kissed Roy on the lips. 'Oh, you just don't know how I've missed you.'

'Me too, 'said Roy, staring into the other man's eyes. The big grin on his face confirming his pleasure.

'You must be Grindal?' said Damien. 'You must excuse us, but it's been a whole week.' He pinched Roy on the cheek.

Grindal stood stock still, mouth wide open. He was speechless. Damien headed toward him. He did not move as Damien gave him a big hug and kissed him on the forehead.

'Poor thing. Roy told me all about what happened.

You must feel really dreadful?' He took Grindal by the hand. 'Now I hope Roy's been looking after you?'

'Er... yes, he's been really good to me,' Grindal replied almost in a whisper.

'Now where are my two little boys?'

'Outside waiting for you,' laughed Roy.

Damien turned his attention back to Roy and proceeded to tell him about his trip as they headed out into the back yard where the two pets had been playing for most of the day.

Grindal's mind was now racing. *Shit, I'm living with two poofters. What a dick head. How could I have been so stupid?* The thoughts flashed through his mind in quick succession. He loathed homosexuals. Repressed memories of a childhood encounter with the local priest tried to push their way into his head. Grindal banished them even before they registered as coherent thoughts. He remembered as a teenager, he and his mates used to bash any arse bandits they came into contact with.

This phobia had stayed with him all his adult life. In fact, it was his considered opinion that they should all be locked up.

Grindal's newfound knowledge about Roy had caught him by surprise. He felt he had been deceived. Yet the man had saved his life. Grindal was confused. The anger rose from the pit of his stomach. It was never too far away from him. Taking a deep breath, he tried to relax.

He watched the two men through the kitchen window. Damien was rolling on the ground with Eric and Mr. Dick the Second, licking his face and jumping all over him. Finally, he picked up the cat, cradling it in his arms like a baby. Roy followed suit with Eric. The pair of them came back into the kitchen all smiles and full of excitement. Like two doting grandparents.

Grindal observed them coolly. Damien was rabbiting on about some carved wooden chest he had bought whilst he had been away.

'It's just gorgeous Roy, you'll love it, I couldn't get it in the car, so I put it on the train. It should be here by four o'clock.'

'Why don't we all go and pick it up and then go for a meal somewhere?' said Roy excitedly. Both men looked across at Grindal expecting an enthusiastic response.

'I might give it a miss,' said Grindal flatly. 'Besides you two lovebirds probably want some time alone.' There was tenseness in his voice that neither of the men seemed to notice.

Grindal excused himself and went to his room closing the door behind him. He sat on the bed staring at the picture of the two naked men. 'Who would have believed it?' he whispered to himself. 'Me, Grindal Falcon living with two brown hatters.'

He looked at the small photograph of Jessie and himself and suddenly felt very much alone. His eyes began to water and there was a lump in his throat. A few seconds passed. He punched the pillow hard.

'Fuck them,' he said out loud.

He knew he would have to leave. The mere thought of being in the same house, as these two perverts made him feel unclean.

He stayed in his room listening to the two men

laughing and talking in loud and sometimes excited voices. His eyes kept wandering toward the picture hanging on the wall. 'I should have guessed, I should have known,' he kept repeating to himself.

An hour passed before there was a knock on the bedroom door.

'Are you sure you won't come with us?' It was Roy.

'No,' Grindal replied flatly.

There was a whispered conversation on the other side of the door that Grindal could not make out.

'All right we'll see you when we get back.'

A few moments later Grindal heard the front door slam. He waited until Roy's car drove away.

The house was silent. He wandered through the rooms. For some reason, he had to confirm the obvious, still not wanting to believe he had been deceived. Roy's bedroom was clearly shared by two people. There were two sets of clothes in the wardrobe. Two bedside cabinets each with various odds and ends that people keep next to their bed. A corkboard hung on the wall displayed numerous photographs of the two men together. Grindal shook his head and wandered back to his own room.

Roy and Damien did not return until much later in the

evening. By that time Grindal was in bed. He tossed and turned for more than two hours wondering what he should do and where he should go. He listened to the muffled voices regularly punctuated with laughter coming from the kitchen. After about half an hour they went into the bedroom across the hallway. A few minutes later Grindal listened with revulsion as the grunts and groans from the bedroom filtered across the hallway. *They're fucking each other*; the thought disgusted him. Mental images of the two naked men flashed across his mind. He wondered who was doing it to who, or did they fuck each other. Grindal buried his head under the bedclothes and tried to think of something else.

The following morning, he took a shower and then ventured into the kitchen. Roy and Damien were already eating breakfast.

'Good morning Grindal, did you sleep well?' asked Damien.

'Yes thanks.'

'You don't look the best, is anything wrong?'

'No, I'm fine, probably the last few days catching up with me.'

'You poor thing,' said Damien. 'Just take it easy for a while. I'm sure things will turn out alright.'

Grindal nodded his head in reply. As he sat eating his breakfast, he couldn't help staring at the two men and thinking of what they had been doing the night before. And yet they seemed so normal, so settled and content with their situation but Grindal could not come to terms with it. The whole scenario played in the back of his mind. Living in a house with two fairies, no way!

'We're going out for the day,' said Roy. 'Would you like to come with us? We're not going anywhere special, just to the city to do a bit of shopping and stuff.'

'No, I'll stay home and take it easy today if you don't mind,' said Grindal.

'Whatever you like said Damien. Maybe you can keep an eye on Mr. Dick? Poor puss has had a bit of a cold and I've been worried about him.'

'Yes, no problems, I'll make sure he doesn't get into any trouble.' *Fancy worrying about a stupid moggy,*

An hour later Grindal had the house to himself. He decided to venture outside to the corner shop and buy a newspaper. As he walked out onto the footpath an old woman was coming from the opposite direction. She stared at him strangely.

'Good morning,' said Grindal.

She looked at the house and then at him and then turned up her nose in an obvious snub. Grindal was surprised by the reaction for a moment but then the thought struck him.

She thinks I'm one of them. He turned and took a step after her wanting to explain he was not one of them he wasn't a poofter. Quickly he realised that such an explanation would be futile and resumed his journey to the shop. 'The sooner I get out of here the better,' he said out loud.

After lunch Grindal decided to check on the pets in the back yard. As soon as he opened the door, the two of them ran inside the house.

'Come here you little sods,' he shouted.

They totally ignored him and ran playfully around the house as he chased them. Grindal did not feel like cleaning up any dog shit so he preferred it if they were outside, even if they were house trained. He decided that the cat would be the hardest to catch so he went after it first. Very soon he cornered it in the hallway. 'Here pussy pussy, come to Daddy,' he mimicked. Mr. Dick eyed him suspiciously and then slipped into the front bedroom. Grindal gave chase and made a final lunge. He missed. The cat in the meantime jumped onto the windowsill and disappeared out of the open window into the front garden.

Grindal quickly changed direction, running out of the front door, he was just in time to see Mr. Dick slipping through the gate which he had not closed properly when he returned from the shop.

'Shit,' mouthed Grindal as he followed the cat through the gate. It was walking slowly down the footpath. Grindal called to him. 'Here pussy pussy.'

The cat turned and then proceeded to cross the road. About three feet from the curbside it stopped. There was a large concrete truck coming in the opposite direction. Grindal held his breath.

'Don't move, don't move', he whispered. If the cat stayed where it was the truck would miss it easily.

Mr. Dick didn't move. Grindal breathed a sigh of relief as it looked as if the truck would pass harmlessly on the other side of the road.

Just as it neared the cat the truck swerved violently catching both Grindal and Mr. Dick by surprise.

'Got the bastard!'

Grindal heard the shout from the open window of the concrete truck as it passed him by. This was followed by a loud whoop of laughter. He looked in disbelief as the truck disappeared down the end of the street.

'You rotten arshole,' he shouted after it as he made a quick mental note of the number plate.

'What will I tell Damien?' In his confused and anxious state, his mind went blank. *Perhaps that's the answer. Don't tell him anything.*

'UBD six four three...UBD six four three.' He kept repeating the number so he wouldn't forget it.

Mr. Dick the Second was flattened. Spread-eagled on the road like a miniature tiger skin rug, eyes staring vacantly into the sky.

'UBD six four three'

There was nothing to be done, Grindal picked up the compacted carcass by the tail, with outstretched arm he walked it back to the house A liquid trail of blood and guts formed a wavy red line on the footpath.

'UBD six four three. UBD six four three.'

He laid the cat on the front doorstep and ran inside to find a pencil and paper. It took him a couple of minutes. He then hurried back outside to where he had laid the dead cat.

'You little sod,' he shouted. 'Get off.'
Eric the dog was snacking leisurely on Mr. Dick's left ear.

'So much for best mates,' said Grindal.

He dropped the pen and notepaper and grabbed the dog. Eric bit him on the hand but he didn't let go until he bundled the squirming dog into the toilet and closed the door. He then went back to the dead cat on the doorstep.

'Now what was that number? UPB nine four three? UBC...? Oh, fuck it.'

He threw down the pen in disgust. Shaking his head and still somewhat bewildered with his predicament, Grindal fetched a large plastic rubbish bag from the kitchen.

'See ya later Mr. Dick,' he mouthed as he dropped the carcass along with several blowflies into the bag.

He buried it in the back yard making sure the hole was deep. He didn't want Eric to turn up on the doorstep with any surprises.

It took Grindal several minutes to wash the doorstep and the path in the front yard. He squirted the footpath as far as the hose would reach to eliminate the tell-tale stains. Finally, he was satisfied that no obvious clues were visible.

When he went to let Eric out of the toilet, he discovered a small pile of dog shit in the corner. By this time, he was passed feeling angry. 'I know how you feel,' he said. This time Eric was glad to get out of the house. Grindal then waited nervously for Roy and Damien's return.

When the two men did return, they were in good spirits; loaded down with shopping bags they had acquired throughout the day.

'Hello Grindal, how are you feeling?' said Roy.

'Good thanks, had a nice long rest this afternoon.'

'How are my two babies?' asked Roy. 'I hope they didn't give you any trouble?'

Grindal coughed nervously. 'Well, as a matter of fact I'm afraid Mr. Dick took it on himself to jump the fence and disappear.'

'Don't look so worried,' laughed Damien. 'He's always doing that, he's probably in heaven at the moment having the time of his life with one of his girlfriends.'

'Yes, I'm sure your right,' he smiled feeling much more relaxed.

Later that evening, Grindal lay listening to giggles, groans and grunts coming from across the hallway. It disgusted him. He knew if he stayed any longer, he might say something that would upset everyone; he made his decision. He would leave the following day. Roy and Damien were going to help a friend move to a new house. He would slip away when they were gone.

The next morning Grindal waited until the two men had left the house. He then took a plastic shopping bag and slowly filled it with his few belongings.

Ten minutes later he was in a taxi heading for a motel he had picked from the yellow pages. On the way he stopped off at the credit union and withdrew some money from his meager savings.

The desk clerk at the Pennington Motel was not very friendly. Grindal had no suitcase, no credit card and was dressed like a circus clown. He paid cash for two night's accommodation. The room was clean and comfortable but at twenty dollars per night he knew his stay there would have to be limited.

The following day he bought a newspaper and turned straight to the accommodation section. Grindal had decided to look for a boarding house that would supply him with bed, breakfast, and evening meal. This, he reasoned would be the cheapest way to live in the short term. His long-term plan was to sell his house block, and maybe rent a small flat somewhere.

There was not much to choose from. He finally decided to try a place in Moonee Ponds. The price was right, and it was not far from Harris Street. Before he went to the boarding house, he visited the local shopping centre and purchased a small suitcase and a few more clothes.

Since he had walked out of Roy's house, Grindal could not shake off a nagging feeling of guilt that he had done the wrong thing. Eventually he dismissed the thought. *Turd burglars deserve everything they get.*

****

CHAPTER 4

The boarding house or gentlemen's accommodation, as it had been advertised, was large and impressive from the outside. It was raised above street level. Access to the front door was gained via a broad stairway enclosed by ornamental brickwork. A wide verandah, which appeared to enclose the whole house, cast shadows over the large windows. Directly opposite the house was what appeared to be a small meeting hall. Grindal could not make out the writing on the signboard, but he did notice it contained a large crucifix. For some reason it looked out of place in the suburban street.

He pressed the doorbell and waited only a few seconds before it was opened by a stern-faced middle-aged woman with bright red hair.

'Yes?' said the woman, without changing her expression.

'I'm looking for room and board, I believe you have some vacancies?'

'That's right, forty-five dollars a week for a share room, fifty-five dollars for a single. For that, you get bed, breakfast and evening meal. No packed lunches and no special menus.'

'Can I have a look at the rooms?' said Grindal. He was not impressed with the woman's sharp tongue, but that didn't put him off. He wasn't looking for friendship, just somewhere to live.

He followed the woman into the house. There was a long passageway with several doors leading off it. He presumed that these were bedrooms but could not be sure because all the doors were closed. She stopped at the end of the passageway and opened the door to one of the bedrooms. It was very large. The walls were painted white, as was the ceiling. There were two single beds at opposite sides of the room. Each bed had its own small cupboard placed next to it. On the wall facing the door there were two wardrobes. The furniture looked very old.

Looks rather bleak, but at least it's clean.

'The other bed belongs to Mr. Boucher. He's away for two weeks,' said the woman.

Grindal thought quickly. If he took this room, he could try the place out for a couple of weeks at the share room price and have the room to himself.

'Well?' said the woman.

'I'll take this room with Mr. Boucher,' said Grindal.

'Right, that'll be two weeks in advance. My name is Fromp, Mrs. Fromp. That's your bed over there.' She pointed to the single bed on the wall away from the window. 'There's a form in the draw next to the bed. Fill out your details on that and give it to me later. House rules are here.' She partly closed the door and pointed to a list of items printed on a piece of white paper which was stuck on the back.

'Read them carefully,' said Mrs. Fromp. 'Anyone who breaks the rules is asked to leave.' She then held out her right hand, palm upwards. 'That'll be ninety dollars in advance if you don't mind.'

He was taken aback by the woman's overbearing attitude and wondered what type of place he was getting himself into. But he had nowhere else to go and his funds were limited so he decided to give it a try.

Slowly he counted out the notes into Mrs. Fromp's upturned palm. When the money had been handed over the hand closed like a rat trap. Mrs. Fromp forced a smile. She then turned and left.

'See you at dinner,' she said without turning; then quickly disappeared through the door at the end of the passage.

'Thanks for showing me around,' said Grindal shaking his head.

He surveyed the austere room. 'I think I might have pulled a real clanger here,' he said out loud.

He closed the door and scrutinized the house rules.

HOUSE RULES

- *No smoking on premises.*
- *No dirty footwear to be worn - ever.*
- *No woman allowed in rooms.*
- *No alcohol allowed on premises.*
- *No foul language.*
- *No personal heaters to be used in rooms.*
- *No personal toiletries to be left in bathroom*
- *No more than 7 minutes allowed under shower.*

Breakfast is served in the dining room between 6am and 7am. Dinner is served at 6pm sharp. Any person who is not seated in the dining room by 6-15pm will not be served. Residents are expected to keep their rooms tidy.

There will be no exceptions to the above rules. Any guests who do not comply will be asked to leave.

E. Fromp
Manageress

Grindal read the house rules and gave a mock salute. He did not envisage staying much longer than the two weeks he had committed to. He consoled himself with the fact that he now had some breathing space, time to plan for the long term. For the rest of the day he found his way around the house and walked down to the corner shop for a newspaper.

There were no other boarders about and as there was nothing forthcoming from Mrs. Fromp, he presumed they were working. The only other person he saw in the house was a young girl who he guessed would be in her late teens or early twenties. She was in an advanced state of pregnancy. When Grindal said hello, she scurried away without replying.

Around 5pm, whilst sitting in his room, he heard the front door open and close several times and presumed that these must be the other boarders coming in from work. Knowing he couldn't avoid introducing himself to everyone he decided to wait until dinnertime and get it over in one hit. The thought of it annoyed him; he hated all that hand shaking rubbish as well as the inevitable questions that went with it.

Grindal went to the dining room at about five minutes to six. He was famished having not eaten since breakfast. He was the first one to arrive and sat himself down at the end of the table. There were five other places set and he wondered whether he had taken anyone's favorite spot.

The first person to arrive was a thin middle-aged man with a hook nose. He looked suspiciously at Grindal then introduced himself.

'Hello,' he said. 'My name's Taff Evans. You must be new around here?'

'Yes, Grindal, Grindal Falcon; I moved in this morning.'

'Well if I were you Grindal I wouldn't sit there, that's Paddy's seat and he's a real arshole, especially when he's been on the piss.'

Grindal was thankful for the advice. He didn't really want an argument with Paddy the arshole on his first night.

'Sit on the other end if you like,' offered Taff. 'That's Boucher's spot but he's not here. Off on his holiday's somewhere; Queensland I think.'

Grindal promptly moved to the other end of the table. 'Thanks.'

As the other boarders entered the dining room. Taff did the honors and introduced Grindal to each one as they sat at the table.

Paddy as his name suggested was a very large Irishman. He merely grunted when introduced. Fortunately, he did not appear to be pissed. There were two men in their late twenties. Dave Jones and Joe Blake were obviously mates. Both looked very fit. Both were relaxed and confident and seemed the type who could look after themselves. The last man to sit at the table was one of those people whose age is hard to pick. Grindal supposed he could have been anything between forty-five and fifty-five years old. He seemed friendly enough and well-liked by the rest of the group. Taff introduced him.

'This is James Crompton, better known as the "Ferret," also known as, the "Love Machine."'

Everyone around the table laughed. Ferret, who was obviously proud of his name, smiled and offered Grindal his hand.

At that moment, Mrs. Fromp entered the room carrying two large bowls of soup. Ferret was served first and received a warm smile along with his soup. He was followed by Paddy, then Taff, Dave and Joe, then finally Grindal. Mrs. Fromp said very little as she served the food. There was no menu yet everyone at the table seemed to know what was coming next. Taff read his mind.

'Monday nights always tomato soup, roast lamb and veg, then apple pie to finish.'

Grindal nodded his head in acknowledgment and wondered what was on the menu for Tuesday. Luckily the food was good and was probably the main reason anyone stayed longer than two weeks.

The Ferret passed small compliments on the food each time he was served. Mrs. Fromp never seemed to tire of it, and always smiled when she served him. Needless to say, he always had a little extra on his plate. The rest of the table exchanged knowing grins each time this little exchange took place, but no one passed any comment.

As the meal progressed Grindal noticed that everyone on the table talked to each other except Taff and Paddy. He had a feeling that there was some kind of rift between the two men and decided he would ask Taff when the opportunity arose. He also noticed that Paddy used the word fuck at least once in every sentence he spoke. It surprised him when he recalled the house rule on foul language. But then he never actually heard him swear when Mrs. Fromp was in the room. Maybe the house rules were not as strictly adhered to as he first thought.

Grindal was both amazed and thankful that no one asked him anything about himself and by the end of the meal he was feeling more relaxed than he had been for some time.

'I'm going for a beer, anyone else?' Taff announced as he rose from the table.

'Might as well,' said Joe. 'Nothing on the telly anyway.'

'You coming Grindal, it's only five minutes' walk?' said Taff.

Grindal almost rejected the offer purely on reflex, but then thought it might be a good idea. He enjoyed a drink and had not had one since leaving Roy's place.

As promised the local hotel was only a five-minute walk. Grindal followed Taff into the bar; being Monday night, it was fairly quiet. The two men sipped on their beer. A short time later, Joe and Dave walked through the door and went straight to the pool table.

'Good lads those two', said Taff. 'Not like that Irish prick.'

'You're not good friends by the sound of it?' offered Grindal.

'Dam right we're not,' said Taff.

At that moment, Paddy walked in the door and looked over towards them.

'Don't leave your fucken change on the bar,' he shouted across. 'There's fucken people around that might fucken steal it.'

'Arshole,' said Taff quietly under his breath.
Paddy walked further down the bar where he ordered a pint and stood alone watching the two men playing at the pool table.

'What's with you two?' asked Grindal.

'It's a long story', said Taff. 'But the long and the short of it is, he reckons I stole some money out of his room. No way. But you can't tell the Irish prick, he doesn't want to know.'

Grindal did not pursue the matter; it was obviously a sore point with Taff. Apart from that, Paddy was twice the size of Taff so any physical confrontation with him was out of the question. He decided to change the subject.

'Where's Ferret?'

Taff smiled. 'Probably choca bloc up Frau Fromp by now.'

'Really.'

'Watch out for the Ferret,' said Taff. 'He'd fuck a dog on a chain. Bars no woman, and very few men. Got a slug on him like a baby's arm.'

Grindal smiled at the description as Taff proceeded to tell him some of the Ferret's amorous escapades. There was also a hint that he may be the proud father of Mrs. Fromp's impending grandchild. It seemed that Meredith, her daughter, had refused to reveal the name of the father. On reflection, Grindal was quite able to believe that Ferret might be the father.

Grindal and Taff stayed in the hotel until ten o'clock then both decided to call it a night. Paddy had not approached them since he came in, he stood at the bar by himself drinking heavily. Grindal walked back to the boarding house with Taff. He was now feeling very tired. There was a chill in the air, and he was looking forward to his bed. As they approached the front door Taff stopped and turned around.

'Hang on a minute,' he said.

Grindal waited and watched in astonishment as Taff walked across the road, looked both ways and then proceeded to let down the back tire of a large black car which was parked in the street.

He ran back across the road wearing a big grin on his face. 'That'll teach the Irish prick,' he said. Grindal did not reply, he was annoyed. He had no intention of getting mixed up in the feud between Paddy and Taff.

After a quick visit to the bathroom he undressed and got into bed. The first thing he noticed was the lack of blankets. It was a cold night and there was no heating in the bedroom. The next thing he noticed, were the lumps in the mattress. After a few minutes of tossing and turning he decided to try the other bed in the room. That turned out to be even worse.

'Fuck me,' he cursed under his breath.

Eventually he settled for pulling the blankets off the unused bed and throwing them back on his own. *At least I'll be warm.* Two hours later he finally fell into a fitful sleep.

The following day he was feeling hung over and tired. After breakfast all the other boarders went off to work. That is all except Paddy who was running late due to a flat tire. To make things worse, his spare was flat which meant he had to go to work by taxi. Grindal stayed out of his way. He had never heard the word fuck repeated so often in such a short period of time.

He decided to go for a walk and explore the local area. After two hours wandering around, he felt tired and went back to the boarding house with the intention of having a nap. When he walked into his room, he was surprised to find his bed was already made. The other bed in the room was now stripped down to the bare mattress. He checked his blankets. There were only two.

'Miserable bitch,' he cursed out loud.

He went straight out of the bedroom in search of Mrs. Fromp. After a quick look around the house, he eventually found her in the kitchen. She was unlocking a padlock that was connected to the fridge door. She did not see him standing in the doorway. He stood and watched her for a moment and wondered whether she kept her money in the freezer, or was she was just a miserable hag. He decided on the latter.

'Can I have a word Mrs. Fromp?' said Grindal. He did his best not to sound annoyed.

She looked up, startled by his presence. 'Yes Mr. Falcon?' she replied, quickly gaining her composure.

'I'd like some extra blankets for my bed if that's possible. I was a bit cold last night and had to use the blankets from the other bed.'

'Yes, I noticed,' she replied with a frown. 'No one else seems to need any extra blankets.'

'That's not really the point is it. Is there a problem with having extra blankets?' He was starting to get annoyed.

Mrs. Fromp picked up on it and quickly conceded. 'All right I'll put some extra on your bed later. Now if you don't mind, I'm busy.'

Grindal left her to the faulty padlock and headed back to his room. He caught a fleeting glimpse of Meredith, Mrs. Fromp's' daughter' as he walked down the passage. But before he could open his mouth to say hello, she scurried away.

Lying on top of his bed he tried to read his newspaper but could not concentrate. He was tired, but too agitated to sleep. The room was cold. But most of all he was lonely. He tried to dismiss his loneliness by thinking of happier times, but this made him worse. It filled him with sadness. The reality of his present situation pushed its way into his thoughts. He had no friends, no money, apart from his old age pension and his house was gone. Logic told him he should clean up the block and sell the land. It was probably worth a few quid. But for some reason he couldn't face the prospect of cutting the final tie to his old life.   He looked around the room.

'What am I doing here Jessie? What am I doing in this fucking dump?' he cursed out loud.

The anger that was always just under the surface of his consciousness came to his aid and swept away the self-pity.

'Fuck it,' he said.

Jumping up from the bed, he left the house and headed down to the hotel where he had been the night before. There, he spent the rest of the day sitting at the bar watching television. After consuming several schooners of beer, his anger eventually subsided. Things looked up slightly when he discovered he could buy a reasonable counter lunch for under three dollars in the pokies lounge.

Around late afternoon the bar began filling up with people as they came in for a drink after work. By this time Grindal was feeling a little worse for wear. He looked at his watch and was surprised to see it was almost dinnertime.

He arrived back at the boarding house just in time. Taking his seat at the table, he listened along with everyone else as Paddy was complaining bitterly about the flat tire incident, he had experienced that morning. He was bleary eyed and had obviously been drinking.

'The fucken bloke at the fucken garage said there wasn't even a fucken puncture. Some fucken bastard had let the fucken tire down. If I catch any fucker fucken about with my fucken car, I'll fucken kill the bastards.'

Grindal looked over towards Taff. He was staring up at the ceiling with his arms folded. There was a lull in the conversation as Mrs. Fromp came in with the soup. She served the Ferret first as she had the night before.

'Mmm thick vegetable, my favorite; you really do spoil us,' said Ferret.

Mrs. Fromp smiled. No one spoke as she served everyone at the table with their soup. Taff seemed to have a problem with a running nose; he was sniffing every few seconds. Grindal looked towards him.

'Hay fever,' said Taff without being asked.

Mrs. Fromp left the room.

'Why don't you blow that shite out of your fucken nose?' said Paddy gruffly. 'It's enough to put a man off his fucken dinner.'

Taff stared across at Paddy and gave a long defiant sniff.

'Fucken idiot you are Taff,' Paddy responded.

The argument didn't go any further as Paddy mumbled something about wanting a fucken piss. He then got up from the table and walked rather unsteadily out of the room.

The moment he had left the room, Taff walked across to Paddy's chair and sat down. Putting his head over the bowl, he held the bridge of his nose with forefinger and thumb, then proceeded to discharge the contents of both nostrils into Paddy's soup. A quick stir with the spoon, and the deed was done.

There was silence for a moment as the rest of the table stared in disbelief.

'You fucking animal Taff,' said the Ferret.

Joe and Dave were laughing they thought it was hilarious. Grindal said nothing. He was neither amused nor revolted. He knew Paddy would murder Taff if he ever caught him carrying out these little acts of sabotage.

Paddy walked back into the dining room and took his seat. All eyes were glued on him as he took his first spoon full of soup. He swallowed it down hungrily.

'Mmm it's got a nice fucken tang to it tonight, must be something special in it.'

Everyone at the table groaned. 'Oohha.'

'What's the matter with you fucken lot,' said Paddy through a mouthful of thick vegetable soup. He was too drunk and too hungry to worry about the groaning and the head shaking around the table.

Grindal looked towards Taff. He had a wide grin on his

face.

'Glad to see you cleaned out your fucken nose Taff', said Paddy across the table.

The wide grin went even wider. There were more suppressed groans from around the table. Needless to say, Paddy was the only one to eat all of his soup. No one enjoyed the rest of the meal. Mrs. Fromp was surprised to see all the food left on the plates. But as no one complained, she made no comment.

Grindal excused himself and returned to his room. He was now feeling totally washed out. He had consumed a lot of alcohol that day and all he wanted to do was sleep. He checked out the blankets on the bed and found that there was one extra. He was not impressed. The room already felt cold and he knew it would get even colder before morning. Grindal resolved to buy himself a small electric heater that he would hide in the bottom of his wardrobe. At least then he could warm up the room each night before he went to sleep.

******

CHAPTER 5

The rest of the week passed slowly for Grindal. The days were long with not much to do and nowhere to go. He tried not to spend too much time in his room it made him feel lonely. At least with his heater he was now a lot warmer. He read two different newspapers, one in the morning, and one in the afternoon just to try and create some kind of routine, some kind of belonging to something.

When Saturday came around, he was glad to spend a few hours in the hotel with Taff. Apart from his complaints about Paddy, he was good company and above all made Grindal laugh. When they arrived back at the boarding house for dinner, everyone around the table seemed to be in good humour. Even Paddy was more agreeable than usual. Grindal looked at his watch. It was six twenty and still no soup.

'I wonder what's happened to the food. Not like Mrs. Fromp to be late,' said Dave.

'I wish she'd hurry up, I'm fucken starving,' said Paddy.

Suddenly there was a loud scream which came from the direction of the kitchen. This was followed by lots of shouting and swearing.

'Sounds like Meredith and her Mum are at it again,' said Taff.

'So much for the house rule about swearing,' replied Grindal.

The shouting began to get louder. There was the sound of heavy footsteps running down the hallway.

Suddenly, the door to the dining room burst open. The heavily pregnant Meredith ran through the door with Mrs. Fromp in hot pursuit. Meredith ran to the end of the table and wrapped her arms tightly around the Ferret. He stood up quickly, a look of shock and disbelief on his face. A glass of water he had been drinking tipped down the front of his trousers and smashed as it hit the floor.

'James, James, I've told her everything. I told her we love each other and we're going to get married. Stop her James before she hurts our baby.'

Meredith was frantic. Standing behind the Ferret she clung onto him tightly, pinning his arms to his sides. Mrs. Fromp now stood inches away from Ferrets face.

'You two timing dirty little bastard,' she screamed at him.

He just stared into the angry face of Edith Fromp. His mouth was wide-open, but nothing came out. For one of the few times in his life the love machine was speechless.

Edith Fromp's face was bright red and contorted with anger. Purple veins bulged in her neck. Without warning, she suddenly brought up her knee and crashed it hard into the Ferret's crotch. He let out a sharp gasp of air. Unfortunately for the Ferret, Meredith was still holding him up with arms pinned to his sides.

Grindal watched as Mrs. Fromp clenched her fist and slowly pulled her arm back. There was a dull thud as the angry blow caught the Ferret square on the end of his nose. The force of the blow sent both him and Meredith careering across the room. Luckily for Meredith she fell back into an armchair in the corner. The Ferret was not so lucky; he spun off to one side and hit the wall before falling to the ground like a wet sandbag. His body was limp. He was out cold. Mrs. Fromp was still not satisfied. She vented the rest of her anger on the inert torso.

'Bastard, bastard, bastard,' she screamed as she kicked the lifeless form with all the strength she could muster. Fortunately for the Ferret she was wearing a pair of soft shoes and was no football player.

The whole scenario had only taken a few seconds. Grindal along with the rest of the boarders was still in shock. Dave was the first one to move. He grabbed Mrs. Fromp from behind and tried to restrain her.

'That's enough now, you'll kill him,' he shouted.

'I'll kill the bastard alright,' she shouted back.

Dave lifted Mrs. Fromp's feet off the ground and physically carried her, still screaming, out of the room. Meanwhile Meredith was now straddled across the Ferret trying to revive him. His nose was bleeding profusely but there were low groaning noises coming from his mouth. The fact that he was alive seemed to take some of the tension out of the situation. Paddy lifted him into the armchair. He pulled a hip flask out of his back pocket and tried to pour the contents down the Ferret's throat. Grindal grabbed all the paper serviettes from the table to try and stem the bleeding.

The Ferret was reviving quickly and beginning to feel the pain in his groin. The tears were rolling down his face as he doubled up in the chair. Every man in the room felt for him. They did not have to guess the pain he was now suffering.

Meredith sobbed as she stroked the Ferret's brow. The eye makeup she had been wearing ran down her cheeks leaving a wavy black line. Her hair was ruffled. She looked a mess.

Grindal looked at Meredith and felt both pity and sadness. She did not have much going for her. He hoped the Ferret would do the right thing by her. His instincts told him he wouldn't. A mother like Edith Fromp made things even worse.

'Out you bastard.'

Grindal was launched back into the present by the angry cry of Edith Fromp as she stood in the doorway. She was carrying a suitcase and an armful of clothing. She marched down the passage, opened the front door and flung the suitcase and clothing out onto the verandah. She then went back to the Ferret's room and proceeded to collect everything he owned. All of it was dumped unceremoniously through the door.

'Come on, you filthy pig,' she shouted from the front door.

Grindal assessed the situation as being potentially dangerous. It was none of his business, but he decided to take control before things got out of hand. The way Mrs. Fromp was carrying on she might decide to arm herself with a blunt instrument and do some real damage.

Dave used the phone in the kitchen to call an ambulance.

'Better to get him out of here before she kills him.' Shouted Grindal as he walked down the passage towards the front door.

'Get that fucking animal out of my house or I'll cut

83

his balls off.'

Mrs. Fromp was still steaming and in Grindal's opinion, potentially explosive. He moved past her and went outside. The ferret's clothes were strewn all over the verandah. Grindal picked up the empty suitcase and proceeded to collect the clothing and place it inside. By the time he had collected everything, the shrill sound of the siren from the ambulance could be heard as it came down the street.

As the driver jumped out, Joe and Dave appeared at the doorway carrying the Ferret between them. Mrs. Fromp was still trying to get at him, and the two men tried desperately to fend off the blows she was aiming at the Ferret's head. The two men in the Ambulance assessed the situation correctly as some kind of 'domestic', and quickly bundled the Ferret into the back of the van.

Meredith staggered out of the house helped by a violent push from her mother.

'You can go too, you filthy slut, and good riddance.' screamed her mother.

Grindal helped her into the back of the Ambulance. Meredith was still crying as she seated herself on the bench next to the groaning Ferret.

As the ambulance sped away Mrs. Fromp gave a last

defiant cry.

'Bastard.'

She then turned and disappeared into the house.

Grindal walked slowly back into the house. His shoes were covered in mud from the flower garden. They left a trail of brown footprints down the hallway. Joe, Dave, and Paddy were talking together in the dining room. Taff was sitting in the armchair looking very white in the face. Mrs. Fromp was nowhere to be seen.

'I knew his dick would get him into real trouble one day,' said Dave.

'Serves him fucken right. He should have thought about that before he started fucken about with young Meredith,' replied Paddy.

'A standing prick has no conscience,' Dave interjected.

Taff stood up from the chair. 'Fuck him anyway, serves him right.'

'And I'm fucken starving,' said Paddy.

'You'll get no fucken dinner here tonight,' said Dave dryly.

'What's the point, let's go to the pub and get something to eat,' said Joe.

They trouped in single file out of the door leaving Grindal standing alone in the dining room. The house was now quiet. He looked at the broken glass under the table and shook his head. He didn't know where to find the brush and pan anyway.

Instead of going to the hotel, Grindal went to the local delicatessen. It was run by an old Greek and doubled as a café for simple meals. He ordered bacon and eggs and ate them slowly and watched the locals as they came in to buy their bread and milk. He thought about the events of the evening. He was no prude but felt an inner loathing for the Ferret. He had destroyed two people's lives just to appease his own selfish sexual appetite. Grindal was certain he felt nothing for either Mrs. Fromp or her daughter. He sympathized with both of them but was glad he was not directly involved in the situation, he had too many problems of his own.

Boucher, the person whom he shared his room with would be back within the next couple of days. He knew without even meeting the man that he didn't want to share with anyone. This left him with two options. He could move into the Ferrets room and stay on. That would definitely be vacant. Or, he could move out. Neither proposition appealed to him. It was not that he liked the boarding house and its inhabitants, it was more the fact that he didn't want the hassle of moving again so quickly. He decided to sleep on it and make his decision the following day.

When he returned to the boarding house, everything was quiet. He presumed the rest of the boarders were still at the hotel. It was freezing cold in his room so Grindal decided to leave the electric radiator on while he slept.

The following day was Sunday. Breakfast was served in the dining room as usual. Mrs. Fromp gave no indication whatsoever that anything unusual had happened the previous night. Grindal was astonished she could look so unperturbed after the violent episode with the Ferret. But then what choice did she have? Taff had telephoned the hospital to enquire after the Ferret. He found out from the ward Sister that he had a broken nose and his testicles were the size of two soccer balls. Apart from that, he was feeling awful.

After breakfast, everyone drifted out of the dining room. Grindal was the last to leave. As he left the room, something caught his eye at the top of the hallway. He turned just in time to catch a glimpse of Meredith peeking through the kitchen doorway. She closed the door quickly. Grindal smiled to himself. He was glad she had come back. He reasoned she was a lot better off with her mother than she was with the Ferret, even though she was a miserable old bag. Anyway, it was none of his business, thank Christ.

The weather was mild and Grindal took a slow walk to

the local newsagent. The Sunday paper was something he enjoyed. On his return he decided to sit on the verandah and read the paper. There was a small table and a few chairs overlooking the street. He made himself comfortable and was soon engrossed in his newspaper.

After about an hour his attention was attracted by movement in the street. People were arriving at the hall across the road. It looked like they were going to a church service. Grindal watched them. They were all dressed in their Sunday best. All smiling and gushing, pretending they were glad to see each other. He had no time for religion or the people that pushed it.

'Bunch of wankers,' he said to himself.

As he observed them, his mind drifted back to the argument that had caused the rift between his daughter and himself. She had become obsessed with some religious group to the point where it had caused her marriage to break up. Her husband Frank had a similar opinion as himself towards religion. Clare was determined not to let go of her new-found Heavenly Father. She was stubborn just like her earthly father. Grindal had taken the side of Frank who he liked a great deal. This he had later regretted, but the damage was done. He had not spoken to his daughter for more than three years. Even at Jessie's funeral they had ignored each other.

Grindal was tired, he had not slept well lately. He closed his eyes, and, in a few moments, he was sound asleep.

The next thing he heard was the sound of a vaguely familiar voice.

'Dad......Dad, are you all right?'
Grindal blinked his trying to focus on the face before him. He was taken totally by surprise when he recognised the face.

'Clare, is that you?'

'Yes Dad.'

'What are you doing here? How did you know where I was staying?'

'I didn't, I was coming out of the church after the service and saw you sitting here. You looked a bit strange, so I thought I . . .' Clare was confused. This unplanned meeting with her father had surprised her as much as it had surprised him. She knew that one wrong question or pronouncement might end the chance meeting almost before it had begun.

'There's nothing wrong with me, I'm fine.'

Grindal was abrupt with his reply. He saw the reaction it had in his daughter's face, and immediately regretted being so abrasive.

'Look, Clare, I'm fine. You don't have to worry about me.' He spoke much softer this time but did not look her in the eye.

She sat next to him at the table. 'I tried to telephone you last week, but the phone was disconnected. I went to the house and saw what had happened and I thought . . .'

Her voice trailed away. Finding the right words seemed to be impossible. She wanted so much for it to go well. For a few long seconds neither of them spoke.

'What do you want Clare?' said Grindal finally.

She took an audible deep breath. 'I want us to be a family again. I want you to come and see the kids. You're their Grandfather. They don't have any other family, and I don't want them to miss out on an important part of their life just because of our argument.' Some of the tension left her. At least now she had told him what she had been feeling for such a long time.

Grindal could detect the intensity in her voice even though she was trying not to be emotional. It was another chance. Something he needed probably as much as his daughter. And yet still he hesitated. His pride already surfacing.

'If you'd listened to me in the first-place things could have been different.'

'But Dad, all I want is a new start. Not a re-run of the past.'

Grindal looked at his daughter. She was staring

vacantly at the newspaper on the table. Her eyes were red, and her bottom lip was quivering. The morning sun went behind a cloud and cast a shadow on her face. In those few seconds, he saw her as she was all those years ago when, as a child she used to sit beside him and share her problems. His pride dissolved in an instantaneous realization of his own selfishness and stupidity.

He took her hand in his and squeezed it tightly. She turned to him, looked into his eyes and knew immediately it was going to be all right. Suddenly they were embracing. The tears were streaming down her face. Grindal held his daughter as he had not done so for many years. He too wept silently.

Soon they were both smiling. They had so much to say to each other yet in the aftermath of the reconciliation neither knew where to start. Clare did not want to engage her father in any questioning that might open up old wounds. She was happy that they were now reconciled and silently thanked God for the divine intervention she had prayed for.

'How long have you been here?' She asked him.

'About two weeks.'

'Do you like it?'

'Not really. The woman who runs the place is a bit of a dragon and there are a few strange people here

'Will you stay?'

'I don't think so.'

'Where will you go?'

'Don't worry, I'll find somewhere.'

There was a short pause as they were interrupted by an agitated Mrs. Fromp.

'Can I speak to you when your guest has left Mr. Falcon.' Grindal nodded in assent.

Clare looked at him and rolled her eyes. 'I see what you mean.'

She waited until Mrs. Fromp had left.

'What happened to the house?'
'Just a stupid accident. My own fault. I was lucky I wasn't killed in the fire.'

'Oh Dad, I'm so sorry. I know how much it meant to you and Mum.'

Grindal grimaced. 'Ah well, that's the way it is. Nothing to be done about it now.'

He then changed the subject displaying the fact that he did not want to discuss the fire. 'How are the kids?'

'Really good. Josh will be leaving school at the end of this term. Says it's a waste of time. He wants to do a plumbing course at the local Tafe college.

'Never was much of a one for school, was he?' Grindal

smiled.

'Kate's in year four now. She's a real bundle of energy. And full of mischief too.'

'They probably don't remember much about me?'

Before Clare could reply, they were interrupted by a man on the pavement. He nodded to Grindal and smiled at Clare.

'Be there in a minute Gerry.' The man wandered off down the street. 'That's my friend Gerry?' Said Clare in explanation. 'He brought me to the service this morning.'

Grindal nodded and smiled. Although he was interested who this Gerry character was, he was determined not to be nosy or interfering.

Clare took a deep breath. 'Why don't you come and stay with us next weekend? We can catch up on what's been happening to each other for the past three years.' Clare smiled but underneath she was extremely nervous.

Grindal was surprised by the offer. 'I couldn't do that Clare. I don't want to cause any more problems between us.'

'Don't be silly Dad, it's just for a couple of days. Josh and Kate will really enjoy it.'

'Anyway, your place is too small,' said Grindal.

'There's a spare bed in Josh's 'room. You can share with him. I'm sure he won't mind.'

Grindal could see that Clare was determined and enthusiastic about the idea. He decided not to spoil the day by directly refusing her offer.

'Alright Clare, I'll think about it.'

Clare beamed. 'Here's our telephone number, just in case you've lost it. Give me a ring and tell me when you're coming.' She hesitated realizing she had been carried away by her own eagerness. 'Anyway, besides that, what about coming for dinner on Wednesday night?'

Grindal smiled. 'What time?'

'Is six thirty all right?'

'Six thirty is fine.'

Gerry was again hovering in the vicinity looking hopefully at Clare. She acknowledged him and stood up.

Grindal and Clare gave each other a big hug before they parted.

'I'm really happy Dad.' She smiled as she walked away.

'So am I Clare.' He waved goodbye as he watched his daughter climb into a car which was parked opposite the boarding house.

'Happier than I have been for three years,' he said to himself.

As he walked back into the house, he was accosted by

Mrs. Fromp. 'Mr. Falcon, when I was doing your room this morning, I found an electric heater. Are you aware of the house rule regarding electric heaters?'

'No,' he lied.

'The rule is quite clear. No electric heaters are allowed. Apart from the untold amount of extra electricity you are using, they are also a fire hazard.'

'So'?

'Normally you would be asked to leave immediately. However, because of recent upsets, on this one occasion I'm willing to let the matter drop. But be warned, if I find you using it again, you'll be out.'

'What you really mean is, you don't want to lose two paying guests in as many days. If you were less miserable and heated the place there'd be no need for electric heaters. Apart from that, the way this place is going you're lucky to have anyone here to break your idiotic rules anyway.'

Grindal walked away without waiting for a reply. 'Stupid woman.' He made sure the remark was loud enough for her to hear. Mrs. Fromp looked very angry. Her mouth was wide open, but no sound was coming out.

He went straight to his room and slammed the door. Although it was quite warm, he immediately turned on the heater. His annoyance increased when he realised he had left his unfinished newspaper outside.

'I bet she fucking steals it,' he said to himself.

Sure enough, when he went outside a few minutes later, the newspaper had disappeared.

To calm himself down he went for a long walk. It gave him time to think about the unexpected meeting with his daughter. By the time he reached the park some two kilometers from the boarding house, he was feeling much better. The prospect of a new beginning with Clare and contact with his grandchildren was something he had not previously contemplated. Now it was a reality. He was determined that miserable Mrs. Fromp would not spoil his day.

He did not return to the boarding house until late in the afternoon. When he walked into his room, he was totally startled to find a naked man looking under the spare bed. The huge backside and hairy scrotum in full view looked grotesque. The man stood up when he realised someone had come into the room.

'Hello, I'm Sid Boucher.' He offered Grindal his outstretched hand. 'You must be Grindal my new roommate.'

Grindal shook the man's hand and nodded. He was still coming to terms with the meeting. Boucher was not very tall, but he had an enormous stomach that hung like a bag of wheat attached to his waist. He wore glasses with thick lenses. His smile displayed large yellow teeth which protruded from his open mouth. Grindal perceived him to be about forty years old but with a figure and face like a sunken blancmange it was difficult to tell.

'I'll come back in a minute when you find your clothes,' offered Grindal.

'Don't mind me,' said Boucher. 'I'm always fairly casual when it comes to wearing clothes. You'll soon get used to it.'

Grindal nodded his head. 'Oh yes, I'm sure I will.' *But only until I move out.* He decided the time had come to start looking for a new place immediately. Grindal assessed Boucher as the type of person who lived in a world of his own, someone who did not give a stuff what other people might think of him.

He went over to the wardrobe to change his shirt. Sid was sitting on his bed picking his nose with his right hand and scratching his balls with his left.

'I see your ambidextrous too,' said Grindal under his breath.

'Beg yours,' said Sid.

'I see it's going to rain tomorrow,' said Grindal.

'Yes, terrible isn't it. Not like Queensland. I was on the

beach every day. Chatting up the girls, going for a swim. Terrific it was.'

'Did you win any hearts?' asked Grindal.

'As a matter of fact, no,' said Sid. 'I can't understand it. I even bought some new bathers for the trip.' He stared inquisitively at something he had just retrieved from his nose.

'Yes, that's really strange.'

Grindal walked out of the room leaving Sid still sitting on the edge of his bed. *I wouldn't share a room with him for free.* He looked at his watch and decided there was just enough time to walk to the newsagent before dinner. He decided to start searching the papers immediately for somewhere else to stay.

After dinner Grindal joined Taff at the hotel for a couple of hours. When he returned to the boarding house, Sid was already in bed. Or to be more accurate on the bed. Still, with no clothes on.

'Hello,' he said cheerfully. 'Do you mind if I read for a while?'

'No, go ahead.'

Grindal went to the bathroom. When he came back to the bedroom, Sid was reading what looked like a pornographic magazine. He had an erection and was looking very excited.

'For fucks sake,' said Grindal.

Sid appeared not to hear the comment; he was totally engrossed in his magazine. Grindal jumped into bed and faced the wall. He was not tired and the thought of someone else in the room made him feel uncomfortable. He tried to analyze this emotion. Was it because Sid was ugly and uncouth? Or, was it because he had not shared the same room with another person for so long?

His thoughts were suddenly interrupted by the sound of grunting noises. He turned around to see Sid masturbating frantically in the bed opposite. Holding the magazine in one hand and his dick in the other, he was arching his head back trying to stop his glasses from slipping off the end of his nose. It seemed the particular picture he was looking at was a very important part of the activity.

Grindal watched the performance. 'What a wanker,' he said. Then started laughing at his own joke. The whole situation was just too ridiculous for words. He was laughing so much he had to sit up. Sid was oblivious to the hilarity coming from the other side of the room. His grunting became more impassioned as he reached his climax.

Suddenly it was all over. A last grunt followed by a long sigh, and then complete silence. Grindal too stopped his laughing at exactly the same time as Sid reached his orgasm. It was as if the laughing and the masturbating were somehow connected. Sid now lay silent and motionless on the bed like a beached whale. Grindal stared at him for a moment. He was filled with a feeling of disgust. The emotion confused him. After all, why should he be worried about someone masturbating? He had done it often enough himself. Perhaps it was Sid's total lack of discretion. He shook his head. 'Definitely, time I moved on,' he said softly to himself.

******

The next two days passed in relative boredom compared with the previous week. Grindal could not get used to seeing Sid wandering naked around the bedroom. He suggested to him that he might find some satisfaction in joining a nudist club. Sid agreed but explained that he was frightened he might be walking around with a hard on all the time. Whilst that didn't bother him, maybe the other members might not find it acceptable. Grindal couldn't argue with that and decided to stay right out of Sid's social life.

When Wednesday came around Grindal was excited. The prospect of visiting his daughter and meeting his grandchildren after such a long time was quite daunting. He had pictured the event in his mind many times over in the past few days. He decided it would be appropriate to purchase a small gift for each of his grandchildren and perhaps some flowers for Clare.

He set out just before lunch and headed for the local shopping centre. He had no idea what to buy for either of his grandchildren and agonized for hours trying to find something suitable. In the end, he decided to buy a bunch of flowers and a large box of chocolates to share between everyone.

When he returned to the boarding house, he was hot and tired. It was early afternoon and the other boarders were still at work. Grindal decided to take a shower. As he stood under the steaming hot water, he tried to relax. He was annoyed with himself for being so uptight. After all he was only visiting his daughter. But still he worried. The nagging thought he might say or do something to upset everyone. He breathed deeply and tried to clear the negative thoughts from his head.

Suddenly the steaming hot shower turned into a cascade of ice water. The shock of the change in temperature made him shout as he leaped from the shower cubicle.

'Faaack'.

There was a hammering on the bathroom door as Grindal wrapped the towel around his shoulders.

'No more than seven minutes under the shower. Read

the rules.' An angry Mrs. Fromp shouted through the door.

'You fucking bitch.'

Grindal was suddenly incensed as he realised that it was Mrs. Fromp who had turned off the hot water. Not worrying about the fact that he was naked he wrenched open the door and came face to face with a very sour looking Edith Fromp.

'What the fuck do you think you're doing?'

'Don't you swear at me, you stupid old bastard. That's against the house rules too. Can't you read?'

Grindal was seething, he was so angry. He placed his hands on Mrs. Fromp's shoulders and shouted into her face.

'House rules.... I'm sick of you... and your house... and as far as I'm concerned you can stick your house and your rules up your big fat arse.'

'How dare you speak to me like that? You're not even dressed. Take your hands off me, you filthy pervert.'

Grindal looked down and was suddenly aware of his nakedness. He turned and went back into the bathroom.

'Get fucked, you old bag.'

He slammed the door in her face.

'Get out of my house. Get out of my house immediately or I'll call the police,' screamed Mrs. Fromp.

'Gladly,' shouted Grindal through the door.

'And don't you dare touch any of my stuff.'

Grindal had visions of his clothes being thrown out into the front garden.

He was still furious and dried himself quickly. When he left the bathroom, Mrs. Fromp was nowhere to be seen. He stormed into his room and threw all of his belongings on the bed. 'Fucking bitch, fucking bitch,' he repeated over and over to himself as he stuffed the clothing into his suitcase.

Within five minutes he had everything together. With his suitcase, the bunch of flowers he had bought for Clare, and the electric heater, his hands were full. He dropped the electric heater as he tried to open the door. 'Fuck it,' he said. Grindal placed his belongings on the bed whilst he plugged in the heater and left it turned on full.

As he walked out of the front door, he bumped into Sid coming the other way.

'Hello,' said Sid. 'Going somewhere?'

'Fuck off wanker.'

He pushed past Sid and stormed up the street suitcase in one hand and the bunch of flowers in the other.

Feeling totally frustrated and still unable to control his anger he held the flowers out in front of him. It was as if the outburst had somehow soiled them. In a fit of total exasperation, he thrust them into the litter bin as he passed the local delicatessen.

As Grindal walked further, his anger began to abate. He breathed deeply and tried to clear his mind. Not far from the boarding house there was a small park. More by reflex rather than intention, he made his way to one of the empty benches. There he sat quietly for a few minutes and assessed his situation.

It was too late in the day to look for anywhere else to stay. He decided he would ask Clare if he could stay at her place. It would only be for one night, two at the most, he reasoned. Hopefully he would find somewhere suitable to live the following day. He decided it was only fair that he should telephone her and tell her about his situation. That way, if there was a problem with him staying, he would find out over the telephone rather than on her front doorstep.

It was late in the afternoon when he contacted Clare. She seemed to be quite pleased that he would be staying the night. This made Grindal feel more relaxed about the situation. Luckily, he had worked out the day before how to get to his daughter's house.

******

CHAPTER 6

Two buses and one hour later he arrived. Walking from the bus stop, he turned into Logan Street, where Clare lived. It was late in the day. The sky was overcast and heavy with dark clouds. He stopped abruptly to avoid a coil of dog shit in the middle of the footpath.

The street before him was long and narrow, a straight line which faded at the limit of his vision. The overgrown grass verge which ran parallel to the footpath created lush islands of green between each driveway. Each island supported a single tree. Most were malformed and twisted. Yellow and brown Autumn leaves formed heaps of litter which spilled over into the road creating uneven piles of brown sludge in the unswept gutter. Telegraph poles leaned at odd angles like headless matchstick men joined by drooping overhead wires. A large colourful for sale sign announcing, "Renovators Delight" perched hopefully on top of a leaning fence.

At first glance, all the houses looked alike, mostly weatherboard. Once brightly painted, the colors were now washed out. The faded paint compared with the faded dreams of the people who occupied them. Most by circumstance, some by choice had failed to board the promised gravy train which swept through urban Australia in the mid-fifties. Grindal shivered as it started to rain. The small suitcase he carried suddenly felt heavy.

Number sixty-four was protected by a low brick wall. The crumbling masonry almost cried out for repair, as did the home it fronted. A leaking gutter over the front verandah emitted a constant stream of water which cascaded onto the cracked paving that surrounded the house. The faded paintwork on the facade was peeling like old wallpaper in a damp room. Grindal smiled grimly.

'Welcome to Logan Street,' he whispered to himself.

He took a deep breath, clenched his fist, and knocked firmly on the door. After a few seconds, there was a rattle of keys followed by a loud creaking sound of the opening door.

'Hello, Dad,' his daughter almost whispered.

As Grindal opened his mouth to reply, a large black dog came rushing past his daughter and jumped up, placing its paws on his chest. Grindal fell backwards and landed in the pool of water which had built up beneath the leaking gutter.

'Bruce, Bruce,' Clare shouted as she frantically grabbed the dog by its collar and pulled it back into the house.

Grindal slowly pushed himself back onto his feet. As he did so he pushed his hand into a large coil of dog shit, a mirror image of the one he had seen at the top of the street.

Totally soaked and soiled, Grindal looked around. He spotted the garden tap and proceeded to wash the filth from his coat sleeve. For some strange reason, he felt no anger. He was calm and determined to stay that way. There was no need for false pride. After all he was at his own daughter's house.

Clare re-appeared at the front door minus the dog. She was visibly upset with tears rolling freely down her cheeks.

'Oh, Dad, I'm so sorry.'

She stood there, waiting for the angry retort from her father. It did not come.

'Nice way to greet your dad after such a long time.' Grindal laughed out loud.

The relief on Clare's face was obvious. She smiled. 'Come on in, I promise the dog won't bite you.' Grindal grabbed his suitcase and followed her.

The house was small. The short passage from the front door had a room connecting on either side and led straight into the kitchen. Clare insisted he take off his wet clothes. She handed him a thick dressing gown and then ushered him into the bathroom. Grindal checked his suitcase, luckily the clothes inside were still dry.

Rather than wear the dressing gown, Grindal showered and put on a clean set of clothes. As he left the bathroom he went back into the kitchen. When he opened the door, Clare was sitting at the table talking to his granddaughter. She had dark hair and looked very much like her mother.

As he stepped into the room, she ran over to him and grabbed hold of his hand.

'Are you really my Grandad? she said. She was smiling and clearly pleased.

Grindal smiled back, he had known her as a four-year-old and she had obviously forgotten him.

'Yes I am. You must be Kate?'

A surge of emotion swept through Grindal as he looked down on the smiling face of his granddaughter. He was overcome with a deep feeling of melancholy he had not felt since the death of his wife. There was a lump in his throat and his eyes started to water. He could not understand why he felt such sadness. Perhaps he was sorry for himself. His past and his present seemed to focus on those few seconds as he gazed into the smiling face before him. He looked across at Clare, she could see he was upset.

It was Kate that finally broke the silence.

'I'm sorry Bruce knocked you down, he's really a very

nice dog. It's just that sometimes he gets too excited. I hope you're not angry with him?'

'No, I'm not angry, he looks like a really friendly dog to me,' said Grindal.

'Do you like dogs?' asked Kate.

'Yes, I do,' he lied.

In fact, he hated dogs and cats and all other so-called pets. In his opinion they performed no useful function in society. Like lots of people he had met. They spent their entire lives eating, shiting, pissing, and sleeping, and not much else.

'Why don't you bring Bruce out and introduce him to Grandad properly?' offered Clare.

Kate laughed and ran off to bring out the dog which had been locked in the bedroom.

The dog was useless and stupid. It was totally untrained and would not even sit when commanded. Nevertheless, it was obviously much loved by his Granddaughter and Grindal did his best to shower it with affection.

The rest of the day and into the evening, Grindal spent happily chatting and drinking lots of tea with his new-found family. Clare explained that Josh, his grandson would not be home until later in the evening. He had gone straight to a friend's house after school and would be eating there.

Apparently, Josh was not too keen on the fact that Grindal would be staying for a couple of days, mainly because he would have to share his room. This made Grindal feel somewhat uneasy. According to Clare, Josh had a bit of a temper. Dealing with an angry teenager was not something he was accustomed to. Still, he was determined not to spoil what was turning out to be something very special for him.

At about eleven o'clock, Josh, was still not home. Clare did her best to seem unperturbed but Grindal could see she was worried. He would have preferred to greet Josh before he retired for the night it might be embarrassing for both of them doing the introductions in the bedroom the following morning. However, it had been a long day and he could barely keep his eyes open. He decided to go to bed.

Clare said she would wait up for Josh and convinced Grindal he would be home any minute.

The bedroom was fairly big, it contained a large wardrobe, a dressing table and two single beds placed in opposite corners of the room. The walls were filled with posters of racing cars, and sports stars along with a few other motley individuals Grindal did not recognize. He presumed they must be pop stars or actors. He was happy to find the bed was comfortable and it was not long before he was asleep.

Sometime later he was awakened by the sound of raised voices coming from the kitchen. He did not know whether he had been asleep for two hours or two minutes. It was dark and there was no clock in the room. Grindal could not make out what was being said but he guessed that Josh had returned home and assumed the argument was due to the hour of his return. He hoped it was nothing to do with the fact that Josh was sharing his room for a couple of days with his long-lost grandfather.

Josh made no attempt to keep quiet whilst he moved about the bedroom. Luckily, he had a bedside light which meant the room was still in semi-darkness. Grindal decided to feign sleep and do the introductions in the morning when things were more settled.

The following day Grindal woke early. He checked his watch; it was six a.m. Josh appeared to be sound asleep in the bed opposite. He decided to take a shower and dress before the rest of the house was up and about. The dog caught up with him before he managed to get to the bathroom. He resisted the inclination to give it a swift kick. Instead giving it a sharp tap on the end of the nose as it persisted in jumping up and licking him.

By seven o'clock Clare and Kate were in the kitchen with Grindal having breakfast. Josh was still in bed

111

seemingly oblivious to the shouts of his mother who called out to him every few minutes to get up. Eventually he surfaced. Bleary eyed and disheveled, he walked into the kitchen and sat at the table. At sixteen years of age, he was taller than Grindal, well built, with thick black hair that hung down over his face.

Grindal had not seen him for almost three years. His memory of him was of a tall skinny youth with pimples and short spiky hair. Even then there had never been any real communication between the two.

'You remember Grandad, don't you Josh?' Clare said awkwardly.

Josh looked across the table and nodded but did not speak.

'Grandad will be staying for a couple of days until he finds a new place to live,' said Clare.

'I hope you don't mind sharing your room?' said Grindal. 'I'll try not to get in your way.'

Josh looked across at Grindal and made eye contact for a few seconds before he replied.

'Don't worry about it.'

Grindal could not perceive any malice in the reply and was content with the fact that there was no open revolt to his presence in the house.

Clare worked three days a week in the office of the primary school which Kate attended. Josh met up with his mate who lived at the end of the street and each day they cycled to the high school which was about twenty minutes away. By eight fifteen everyone had left. Clare and Kate on foot, and Josh on his bike.

Grindal was left alone with the dog, which he immediately dispatched to the back yard. He made himself a cup of coffee and sipped it slowly as he listened to the nine o'clock news on the radio.

Later that morning he walked to the local shopping centre and picked up a newspaper. A quick perusal of the accommodation section proved that Thursday was not a very good day to look for a place to live. He convinced himself that there was not much point in looking for anything until Saturday, after all there was no desperate hurry.

Grindal decided to have his mail re-directed to his daughter's house, he had not asked, but was sure she wouldn't mind. Currently it was being held at the post office close to where he used to live. He had not picked it up for some time. With nothing better to do, Grindal decided to go and collect it.

The bus trip back to his old house took nearly two hours. He had to wait at least thirty minutes to make the right connections. The bus-stop at the end of the street where he used to live took him past his old house. Grindal steeled himself mentally as he expected to see the burnt-out ruin. But as he drove past, he was surprised to see the block of land was bare. Slight traces of charred earth, the only remnant of the house where he and Jessie used to live. Grindal was confused. He had not asked anyone to clear the block. No one had been given permission to touch his property.

The mystery was solved when he opened a letter from the local council. The letter had given him fourteen days' notice to clear the block otherwise the council would do it and send him the bill. In another letter dated fourteen days from the first was a bill for one hundred and thirty- four dollars. To be paid within thirty days.

'Fucking bastards,' he said under his breath.

Along with all the other bills in his hand which included final payments for gas, electricity and rates, he was in debt for nearly three hundred dollars. He calculated that he had two hundred and fifty dollars in the bank which left him with a problem. All the accounts he held in his hand were already due for payment. Finding who knows how many dollars rent in advance for new accommodation would make the matter worse.

He had never been any good handling money and

paying bills. Jessie used to do all of that. He now wondered how she ever managed. He shook his head in frustration.

'Fuck the bills,' he muttered to himself.

Pushing the pile of letters into his coat pocket he turned around and headed back to the bus stop. He reasoned there was not much point walking back down the street to look at his now vacant block of land. As he stood waiting for the bus, he wondered how much money the block was worth. He had no idea about real estate. A few thousand, not much for a lifetime of work and worry. He glimpsed the land again on the return journey. This time the empty space made him firstly sad and then angry.

The anger stayed with him until he reached his daughter's house. Not boiling and immanent but smoldering on the edge of his conscious thoughts. He fumbled in his pockets looking for the door key Clare had given him.

As he was about to open the door, he heard a loud scream which came from the house next door. This startled him and he stood motionless trying to decide whether the sound had been real or just in his imagination. A few seconds later there was another scream.

Grindal walked slowly to the low fence which divided the two properties. A swarm of thoughts flashed through his mind. Should he investigate? Should he mind his own business? What if it was a domestic? That would make him look a right dickhead. Then again, someone might be in real trouble.

His instinct told him to mind his own business, after all he had enough problems of his own. Nevertheless, he straddled the low fence and walked slowly and quietly to the rear of the house.

When he reached the corner of the building, he took a cautious look. At the rear of the house there was a pair of glass sliding doors which were open wide. He could hear the sound of breaking glass. As he crept closer to the open door, an angry voice shouted out.

'Where's the fucking money, you old bag?'

'There is no money. Honestly,' came the almost frantic reply.

Grindal could almost hear his heart pounding in his chest. He edged closer and dropped onto his haunches before cautiously looking through the glass door.

There were two people in the room. One was a woman in her mid-sixties. She was visibly shaking. Tears were running down her face and she was whimpering. There was a look of absolute terror in her eyes.

The other person was a tall youth wearing a track suit. He was skinny with short red hair. The thing which held

Grindal's attention, was the long-bladed knife which he waved from side to side in front of the terrified woman.

Grindal pulled his head back. 'Fuck me,' he swore. His hands were shaking he didn't know what to do.

'Maybe I should push this up your fucking nose? Maybe then you might remember where you put the money?'

The angry voice from inside the house triggered Grindal into action. He stood up and walked slowly through the glass doors. The red- haired youth was totally surprised.

'What's your problem son?' said Grindal, looking the youth straight in the eye.

He circled around to the other side of the room leaving an escape route through the open door hoping the youth would flee. His heart was still pounding but outwardly he was trying to appear calm.

'Why don't you just fuck off and that will be the end of it. No police. No problems.' He said the words slowly and firmly.

The youth looked at him weighing up the situation. Some of the tension went from his face.

'You want some of this too grandad,' he said, waving the knife in Grindal's direction. He smiled nervously.

The arrogance of the youth stirred the anger that had been simmering in Grindal's stomach all afternoon. It built up quickly as the smile on the face opposite him, grew more confident.

To his right- hand side placed on the floor was a large pottery urn over two feet tall. Grindal turned quickly picked up the urn and raised it above his head.

'Baas...taard.' He screamed at the top of his voice and charged across the room, straight for the youth. The smile disappeared and his eyes almost bugged out of their sockets.

The menacing scream and the sight of a very large urn bearing down on him made the youth cut and run. Grindal threw the urn with all the strength he could summon just as the youth reached the doorway. The urn missed the youth completely and disintegrated along with the glass door it collided with.

The woman in the house had been frozen with fear up until the time the urn hit the door. At the sound of the breaking glass she let out a high- pitched scream that was so loud it stopped Grindal in his tracks. There was no way he would catch the fleeing youth, nor did he have any inclination to follow him. He watched, as the would-be assailant jumped the garden fence and headed up the street, head down, running as fast as he could. Grindal was relieved to come out of the situation without a knife being stuck into him.

'And don't fucking come back,' he shouted.

The adrenalin was still pumping through his veins.

As he turned around, he was almost knocked off his feet as the woman grabbed him and wrapped her arms around him so tightly, he could hardly move.

'Oh, dear god. Thank you. Thank you.'

She was still shaking and Grindal suddenly felt embarrassed by the situation.

'It's alright now. He's gone. Just calm down,' said Grindal trying to soothe her and collect himself at the same time. Not knowing what else to do he led her back into the house and sat her down on a chair.

'Can I make you a cup of tea or something?' he Offered.

******

CHAPTER 7

Moira Murdoch was a widow. Her husband had been dead for seven years. For the past five of those seven years, she had been looking for someone to spend the rest of her life with. Since the day of the attempted robbery she had decided that both God and fate had combined to send her the partner for whom she had been waiting for so long.

It had been seven days since the event had taken place. In that time Grindal had received several invitations to dinner. Two, home- baked apple pies and a strange looking medallion on a silver chain. 'A token of her respect,' as she had put it to him.

At first Grindal was flattered by the attention he was receiving. This quickly turned to embarrassment when the medallion was presented with great sincerity by a starry-eyed Moira. He had now reached the point where he was frightened to leave the house for fear of being accosted before he reached the front gate.

It turned out that Moira was a great believer in all things metaphysical. At one of their brief encounters over the front fence, she had explained to Grindal that the stars had foretold of their meeting. She was convinced that this was the truth because the Tarot cards and the Runes had confirmed the event a week before. Not, in specific terms of course, as she was careful to explain to him. But the signs were all there.

Grindal was totally bemused by all this talk of runes and astrological predictions. He did not wish to show his ignorance by asking what a rune was, but then it did not really matter. As far as he was concerned it was a load of rubbish. Normally he would have been quick to give his opinion on the subject. But Moira now regarded him as her great protector and even told him as much. Because of this he did not have the heart to tell her what that he thought she was talking a load of rubbish. Instead he feigned a sort of detached interest and excused himself as quickly as possible whenever the mumbo-jumbo entered the conversation. He thought it a great pity that such an intelligent woman had become mesmerized by such nonsense. Aside from that, her home-made apple pies were the most delicious he had ever tasted.

****

Lately Grindal had not been at ease with himself. He had now been staying at his daughter's house for three weeks.

121

When he had explained to Clare about the money he owed the council, she had insisted that he stay longer. Whilst this was not a problem for him, it seemed to be a big problem for his grandson with whom he shared a room.

The problem had been exacerbated to almost breaking point a few days earlier. Grindal had left the house along with the rest of the family first thing in the morning. He informed everyone at breakfast that he would be out all morning inspecting a potential boarding house. As he was waiting for the bus, he had second thoughts about his plans and decided the place he was about to inspect was too far away from his daughters. Instead he went for a short walk and returned to the house an hour later.

When he entered the house, he was surprised to hear laughter and conversation coming from the bedroom. Expecting the house to be empty he cautiously and quietly crept down the short passage to the bedroom. Without any announcement, he burst open the door.

His grandson was there with some girl Grindal had never seen before. Both were totally naked and obviously in the act of having sex. The girl screamed. Josh went bright red before he recovered sufficiently to tell Grindal to 'fuck off out of it.' Then, as he was leaving, he told Grindal he should hurry up and find someone else's house to live in. Grindal apologized for the intrusion and left.

Josh had barely said a word to him since. It was important to Grindal that he have a reasonable relationship with Josh. He liked his grandson and admired his independent attitude. What was at best a cool relationship was now stone cold. Grindal wanted to talk to Josh but did not know how to go about it. He had never had a son. Like most men he sometimes wondered, if he had, would it have made him a different person.

The age difference between himself and Josh only made matters worse. They seemed to have so little in common. Grindal was unable to understand how anyone could prefer the things his grandson seemed to favor. The loud repetitive music, mindless soapie's on the television. Worst of all why did he and his friends wear clothes that seemed to be two sizes too big. Their trousers hung on them like they had shit themselves. The situation depressed him. Deep down he knew it was because he was old, and most of all intolerant, but did not care to admit it. Nevertheless, he was determined to find a way to patch up their relationship. He knew it would mean he would have to move out. But wasn't that always his intention?

That evening Grindal decided to visit the local hotel. He had not been there before, nor had he had a drink for a while. He knew Clare was not in favour of alcohol and respected her wish not to bring it into the house. He presumed it must be some rule or belief of the religious mob she belonged to.

He told Clare he was going out for a walk and she did not ask him where he was going. Grindal presumed she had already guessed. The hotel was about fifteen minutes' walk from the house. It was a cold night and he was glad to get inside. At first, he found himself in the entertainment lounge where a very loud band was playing. The vocalist was shouting some undecipherable words into the microphone. Grindal beat a hasty retreat into the bar. It was still noisy but at least he could hear himself think.

As he stood and sipped his pint of beer, he looked across into the entertainment lounge through the other side of the bar. The room was filled with mostly youngsters who did not look old enough to be there. They all shouted at each other across the tables trying to make themselves heard over the music. Grindal shook his head unable to fathom what mystical insight was required for anyone to enjoy such rubbish.

His mind slipped back to the times when he and Jessie used to go for a drink on a Saturday night. They always used to go to the local RSL. Things were different then. No poker machines, no rock and roll bands. They used to have what they called a sixty forty band which played music you could dance to. And then later in the night everyone would have a sing-along. All the old favorites, good music, real music. He had never really worked out what the sixty forty business meant, but it was certainly better than the crap people listened to today.

Still, like everything else, things changed. New committees, new ideas. Eventually they stopped going. A couple of people in the group they mixed with died unexpectedly. After that it wasn't quite the same.

Grindal was aroused from his reverie by the sound of a voice he recognised. He looked up to see Josh, his nephew, was on the other side of the bar which faced the entertainment room. He was shouting a drink order to the barman. At first, he did not see Grindal, but as he walked away from the bar with a drink in each hand, their eyes met. Josh stopped, as if transfixed by the unexpected meeting. Grindal just nodded his head in acknowledgment. He watched as Josh's face went bright red and his lips mouthed the words 'fuck'.

Grindal watched as he walked away and disappeared amongst the noisy throng sitting near the stage. Josh was angry, he had been sprung drinking in the hotel when he was supposed to be studying at his mate's house. Grindal wanted to shout after him and tell him not to worry. He wouldn't dob him in to his mother. But it was too late. The unanticipated meeting had spoiled the night for both of them. Grindal finished his drink and left.

The next morning, they were all sitting around the breakfast table. As usual everyone except Grindal was in a hurry. Conversation was normally limited to what was essential to get everyone out of the house on time. Grindal noticed that Josh looked red around the eyes, and so did his mother.

'You were late last night Josh, what time did you get in?' asked Clare.

Josh looked directly across at Grindal as he answered.

'I don't know, about eleven thirty.'

Grindal knew it was more like twelve thirty Josh had crept into the room.

'I hope all this studying has some benefit,' said Clare. 'Too much of it is no good for you. You know what happens to you when exams come up. You get up-tight then your mind goes blank and it's all a waste of time.'

Josh dropped his head and stared intently at the bowl of cereal before him.

'Maybe you should relax a bit more,' offered Grindal.

'You know, go out to the milk bar or something.'

'Maybe Grandad's right, maybe you are working too hard,' agreed Clare.

Josh looked across the table. Grindal looked back, winked, and carried on with his breakfast. He did not know whether he had endeared himself to his grandson by not giving him away. Josh said nothing except his usual 'see ya,' as he left the house.

Later that afternoon, Grindal checked the mailbox. Along with the usual bills and circulars, was a letter with his name on it. There was no address and no stamp which meant it must have been hand delivered. He opened it quickly having no idea who it might be from. He had mixed emotions when he read the contents. It was a formal invitation to a birthday party for non-other than Moira Murdoch, his admirer from next door. Grindal shook his head in dismay as he pondered on the type of people he might meet at Moira's party.

'Probably a house full of witches and wizards,' he muttered to himself. He then spent the rest of the day wondering how he could excuse himself from going. After devising a whole host of complicated apologies, he decided to accept the invitation and then feign sickness on the day of the party. He castigated himself silently for not having the courage to say no and be done with it. Maybe he was going soft in his old age.

Grindal mentioned the invitation to Clare that night over dinner.

'The twenty seventh you say. That's a shame,' said Clare.

'Why is that?' Grindal replied, somewhat surprised.

'That's the night I have the church group here. I know you don't believe in anything religious,' she said defensively. 'But I was rather hoping that you might at least sit and listen to the group'.

There was a sudden silence as each member of the family waited for his reply. Clare had been praying fervently for the swift conversion of her atheistic father and was hoping that some kind of miracle might occur at the monthly prayer meeting. The silence seemed to last forever as Grindal's mind went into overdrive.

What a choice. The sickness ploy was now, definitely out, as he visualised Clare's religious group saying a prayer by his bedside for his recovery. Trapped between new age and old age nonsense he had to make a preference.

Knowing himself too well he decided to opt for the witches and wizards. At least if he upset someone with his opinions, it wouldn't be his family.

'Perhaps I should accept Moira's invitation? She might get upset, and after all, it is her birthday. Maybe I can sit in at your meeting next month?'

Clare took his reply as a positive response, if nothing else, she was a very patient person when it came to the will of her god.

'Yes Dad, that might be the best idea. And as you said, you can be involved in our next meeting.'

Grindal noted the 'be involved' comment and wondered what that might entail but decided not to pursue the matter. He was rather peeved by the way he had let himself become trapped. Normally he would dismiss these events without hesitation.

'What will you buy Mrs. Murdoch for her birthday Grandad?' chirped Kate.

'That's none of your business,' broke in Clare, before Grindal could reply.

'That's alright Clare, maybe Kate can suggest something Moira might like.'

'There's no time for that now, let's go, or we'll be late.'

Grindal quickly picked up on his daughter's agitation. She hated being late for anything. For her, punctuality was next to Godliness.

'Maybe we can talk about it tonight,' said Grindal.

'Can we take Bruce for a walk tonight too Grandad?' asked Kate.

'Yes alright, now off you go before Mum gets angry.'

Five minutes later the house was empty. Grindal poured himself a second cup of tea from the large brown teapot. For a moment, he basked in the silence that pervaded the room. His mind switched back to his granddaughter's comment on the present for Moira Murdoch. Suddenly Grindal was touched by a finger of shame. He thought of Jessie. He had never bought another woman a gift before. Even the contemplation of it now made him feel it would be an act of betrayal. The woman he had loved and now missed so desperately, so easily and conveniently tossed aside.

He walked into the bedroom and picked up the treasured photograph of Jessie and himself that sat on the small cabinet beside his bed. He stared at it. It was the catalyst that sent his mind back in time. A mixture of emotions bombarded him as various images cascaded from the memory bank of his mind. And yet as always, the final emotion was one of loss. With it, that desperate sadness that can never be appeased.

Grindal gently replaced the photograph on the cabinet. As he walked from the room, it was anger that pulled him from his perceived vulnerability which was his sorrow.

'Why don't people just fucking leave me alone,' he said irritably.

To calm himself Grindal left the house with the intent of going for a long walk. He needed space, time to think. As he reached the gate a voice from behind made him even more annoyed.

'Morning Grindal, would you like a cup of coffee?'

Moira Murdoch was the last person he wanted to talk to at that moment. He did not respond. Slamming the gate behind him, he walked purposefully up the street.

And yet within seconds his conscience assailed him again. Why had he ignored Moira? It wasn't her fault. She must have been upset and confused by his attitude. Grindal shook his head in frustration.

'Fuck it,' he said out loud.

The long walk did not solve any of Grindal's problems. By the time he returned to the house he was tired and confused. The one thing he did resolve was to go next door and apologise for his ignorance and at the same time accept the invitation to the birthday party. In case he changed his mind Grindal decided to get the apology over with.

He knocked on the door with some trepidation. Moira opened the door almost immediately and smiled.

'Hello,' she said.

'Hello,' he replied. 'I'm sorry I ignored you this morning,' he said awkwardly. 'It was just that I had a lot on my mind.'

'That's all right,' she replied warmly. 'It happens to all of us sometimes. Would you like to come in?'

'Err... no thanks, I have to get going.' Grindal backed away from the door. 'By the way, I'll be happy to accept your invitation.' He felt himself blushing and retreated quickly before she could see his embarrassment.

Later that afternoon when Clare and Kate returned from school, Grindal was reminded of his promise to his granddaughter to walk the dog. They set off almost immediately for the small park which was not far from the house. Kate walked with the dog on a lead. Bruce had long since learned that Grindal was not a dog person and smart enough to know that getting out of line may result in adverse consequences.

'How come Bruce is always well behaved when we take him for a walk Grandad?' asked Kate.

'Beats me Kate. Maybe he just likes our company.'

They walked on until they reached the park. The play equipment was rusted and broken. Swings with no seats and roundabouts that did not go around. They sat on a solitary bench and watched as the dog ran freely stopping frequently to savor any new scents the park had to offer.

'Did you decide what to buy Mrs. Murdoch for her birthday, Grandad?' asked Kate.

'No, not yet. Have you got any ideas?'

'Well, maybe some flowers, or a nice necklace.'

'I don't think grandad could afford a necklace that would be nice enough.

'The flowers would be a good idea though,' replied Grindal.

'What about some flowers and some chocolates,' suggested Kate.

'Now that's a really good idea. Why didn't I think of that? Flowers and chocolates it is.'

With the dilemma of the birthday gift decided, Kate ran off to play with the dog. Grindal watched as the pair chased each other around the park. He had become close to his granddaughter since he had moved into the house. She was never demanding and always had a happy smile for him. He wondered whether the fact that her father rarely visited made her unhappy. He was not yet confident enough to explore this situation with her. Besides, for the past few months he had not done any visiting himself and therefore was in no position to pass judgement or comment on anyone else.

Lately, life for Grindal seemed to be so complicated. He gazed absently at his granddaughter and the dog. Suddenly it occurred him that since Jessie's death he had been made to confront many situations which demanded a reaction. He was no longer insulated by a relationship that posed no questions, no problems. It was the beginning of a new phase in his life. It was a new game and he was not very good at it.

******

The evening of the twenty seventh came along very quickly. The invitation had said seven thirty. Grindal was ready an hour sooner, not for any reason other than Clare's religious group were scheduled to arrive at seven the same evening. He had been convinced by his daughter that it would be good manners to introduce himself before he left. Josh was long gone. Grindal could not understand why he should be involved in the group, yet his grandson got off scot free. He decided he would take the matter up with Josh as soon as the opportunity arose.

Grindal had decided to wear the medallion Moira had given him after the house break-in. It seemed to be rather large as he observed it through the dressing table mirror as it hung on his chest. He had no idea if the design on the medallion stood for anything in particular and reasoned that it must be some kind of good luck charm.

The flowers and chocolates had been purchased and suitably wrapped by his daughter. Grindal had mentally steeled himself for the occasion and was now, as his grandson might put it, "ready to rumble".

Just before seven there was a knock at the door. Clare, who had been waiting in anticipation, quickly went to open it.

'Oh, hello, Gerry, please come in.' Clare promptly ushered Gerry to the sitting room where Grindal was waiting apprehensively to greet the visitors.

'You've already met my father.'

'Yes, very briefly,' replied Gerry. 'Nice to meet you again Mr. falcon,' said Gerry as he offered his hand towards Grindal.

Grindal took his hand and shook it firmly. 'Likewise.'

The two men sat opposite each other and there was an awkward silence as each made nodding and smiling gestures, but neither spoke. Grindal decided that Gerry had been filled in on his religious disposition and was playing it safe. A further loud knock on the door caused each of the men to stand for no apparent reason.

'That must be Brother James,' said Gerry, and immediately went to greet him. Grindal was less enthusiastic and waited for brother James to appear.

Clare brought him into the room a few seconds later. 'Dad, this is Brother James, he's the leader of our group.'

'Grindal shook his hand more firmly than he needed to. 'Is that Reverend James, or just Brother James?' he asked.

'Yes, it is Reverend James, but in our group, we prefer to call each other Brother and Sister,' he smiled.

Brother James was looking suspiciously at the large medallion hung around Grindal's neck.

Grindal looked down at the medallion.

'It's a good luck charm used by witches,'

Grindal smiled back at Brother James, still holding his hand firmly.

'Dad's just joking, aren't you,' said Clare?

She was not sure. The look of tension on her face reminded Grindal that he must not say or do anything stupid. He released his grip and left the question unanswered. Grindal had taken an instant dislike to Brother James, and knew the feeling was mutual.

The Brotherhood of the Second Coming was a fundamentalist Christian group. Clare was deeply committed to her religious beliefs. When her marriage broke up, she became even more committed. A fellow workmate introduced her to the Brotherhood. Since that time Clare had become a staunch member of the group. At the time Grindal had been infuriated, convinced she had been brainwashed at a time in her life when she had been most vulnerable. Still, that was in the past, he now reasoned that he had no other choice than to put up with the situation. He knew his daughter was totally indoctrinated with this religious rubbish but did not want to make her unhappy by being antagonistic towards her group.

As the rest of the Brotherhood came into the house he smiled and shook their hands. By seven fifteen there were ten people in the house, all sat in the now crowded sitting room on the extra chairs he had brought into the room earlier. Grindal looked anxiously at his watch. It was time to go.

'Perhaps Brother Grindal would like to join us in our opening prayer?' announced the group leader.

Clare looked hopefully at her father.

'Sorry, Brother Grindal has to go, maybe next time.' Grindal walked hurriedly to the door. He felt proud of himself for not upsetting anyone. In fact, he didn't even feel angry. Just bemused that a group of intelligent people could waste their time on such nonsense.

The outside air was cool. He looked over the fence and

wondered if it was too early to go to the house next door. He preferred not to be the first to arrive and decided to wait in the shadow of the only tree in the front garden. A few minutes later he listened as the sounds of contrasting music drifted into the front garden where he stood. From Moira's house, Tom Jones sang "The Green Green Grass of Home." The Brotherhood of the Second Coming sang with equal gusto, "Rock of Ages."

Having watched several people arrive next door, Grindal decided it was time to make his entrance. As he knocked on the door, he felt stupid standing there with flowers and a box of chocolates. It suddenly occurred to him that a bottle of wine might have been more appropriate.

The door was opened by a man dressed in a red velvet jacket. This took Grindal by surprise. For a moment, he didn't know what to say. He fumbled with the flowers and the chocolates.

'Hello, I'm Grindal Falcon.'

The man before him raised his hands above his head staring towards the heavens.

'Moira, the hero has arrived,' the man turned and shouted into the room behind him.

For a brief moment Grindal became annoyed when he thought the man was taking the piss out of him. This quickly passed as Moira appeared at the door and rescued him from the strange man in the velvet coat.

'Grindal, how nice to see you,' Moira smiled.

Grindal pushed the gifts he was carrying into her hands, eager to get rid of them.

Moira held the bouquet to her nose.

'You shouldn't... they're beautiful, ... I must put them into a vase. Egor, please introduce Grindal to everyone while I find a vase.'

'Certainly, my dear.'

Moira quickly disappeared as Grindal was ushered into the room full of strangers.

'Can I have everyone's attention?' Egor shouted above the noise.

'Quiet please,' he shouted again.

Someone turned off the music and suddenly all eyes were staring at Grindal and Egor.

Egor made a theatrical bow before presenting Grindal to the group.

'This my friends, is Grindal Falcon. The brave man, who so recently rescued our dear Moira from the clutches of a violent intruder. Probably saving her life and her possessions. And for that we are all truly grateful.'

There was a short silence before everyone in the room

broke out in loud applause.

Grindal was speechless. Egor had joined the rest of the group leaving him standing by himself. Grindal shook his head not knowing what else to do. Luckily Moira came to his rescue pushing a drink into his hand and pulling him off to one side.

'I hope Egor didn't embarrass you,' she said. 'He's my brother, he's also an actor and tends to get carried away with things at times. Actually, his real name is Richard, but he feels the name Richard is much too boring for someone in the theatre.'

Grindal smiled. 'I must admit, he doesn't really look like a Richard.' *Looks more like a Dick.*

Moira took Grindal by the hand and led him towards a group of people who seemed to be studying the upturned hand of a younger woman.

'Come along now don't be shy,' said Moira. 'I must introduce you to Felix, he's one of the best palm readers you have ever met.'

'I've never met a palm reader of any sort,' replied Grindal dryly.

Moira was not fazed by his reply. 'Then here's a golden opportunity for you,' she smiled.

Felix was a very intense individual who obviously took

his palm reading seriously. When Grindal entered the group, everyone smiled and said hello. Moira reeled off their names which he immediately forgot. She then excused herself and left him standing in the small cluster staring at the upturned palm.

'This is just a fun reading,' Felix assured him. 'No dark secrets or anything private.'

The girl with the upturned palm smiled at Grindal. He decided to say nothing he was not impressed. He decided to find another drink before he was tempted to give an opinion on the reading. The glass of wine Moira had thrust into his hand tasted sour. Grindal had never been able to acquire a taste for wine, what he really needed was a glass of beer. As he turned to leave the group, Felix addressed him.

'Would you like me to do yours Grindal?'

'No thanks, replied Grindal. 'I think I'll give it a miss this time if you don't mind.'

'That's a very large Ankh you've got there,' said Felix.

Everyone stared down at Grindal and nodded in agreement. The comment made Grindal uneasy, mainly because he had no idea what an Ankh might be. He looked down at himself and wondered for a moment if they were trying to tell him his fly was unzipped.

'The chain matches nicely,' said an elderly woman in

the group.

Realization dawned on him instantly. 'Yes, it is rather nice. Moira gave it to me.

'What exactly is an Ankh?' asked the young girl in the group.

Grindal froze. He knew if he made something up he would be caught out. Saying nothing would be worse. A small streak of anger flashed across his mind. He suddenly felt cornered. Who were these bunch of dickheads asking him about a dopey medal? *I'll tell them what a wank is in a minute.*

'It's a symbol of life, used by the ancient Egyptians.' Moira's voice came from behind him. Grindal smiled and nodded his head in agreement. He wondered if anyone in the group had noticed the unspoken change in his emotions.

'Scuse me, I must top up my drink. Moira would you have any cold beer?'

He turned and retreated from the group. Moira followed behind him.

'Where are you going?' she asked. 'The beer's this way.'

Grindal turned around. Moira was smiling and pointing towards the kitchen. Grindal followed her to the refrigerator. A long swig of the ice-cold beer made him feel more relaxed.

'What's the matter?' asked Moira. You look a bit tense.

'I suppose your right,' said Grindal. 'I'm a bit like a fish out of water. I don't really understand any of this New Age business. I know your keen on it, but I must be honest with you. I don't believe a word of it. And that's putting it nicely coming from me.'

'Never mind about that,' she smiled. 'I promise I won't leave you on your own again. Come on.'

She took him by the arm and marched him back into living room. As he walked beside her a vision of Jessie flickered before him, and with it came a strange feeling of guilt.

Moira stayed with Grindal for most of the evening. When she had things to do for her guests, she asked Grindal to help out. This suited him perfectly it prevented him from being drawn into any unwanted conversation. Grindal was happy to find out that most of the people in the room were quite ordinary. Not all witches and wizards as he had first thought. In fact, half of them were from the lawn bowls club that Moira went to.

Later in the evening they sat together on the sofa. Grindal was now on his fifth beer and was feeling much more relaxed than he had been earlier on.

'I hope some of that tension is beginning to disappear,'

said Moira.

'Yes, it is,' replied Grindal. 'Mainly thanks to you. He leaned back on the sofa and stared vacantly at the ceiling. 'Since my wife died, I've had a few problems. I always was a bit of a grump. But now . . . The slightest upset seems to make me boil inside.'

'Yes, I heard about some of your problems from Clare, it must be awful for you. No one could blame you for being easily upset at the moment. I'm sure that things will improve as time passes,' said Moira.

'That's what I keep telling myself,' replied Grindal. 'The problem is, it seems to be getting worse. Maybe I'm going crazy,' he laughed.

'Tell you what might be a good idea,' said Moira. 'Why don't you come with me to this new class I've enrolled for?'

'Class, what kind of class?' asked Grindal.

'Well, ever since the break in, when you rescued me,' said Moira as she took hold of Grindal's hand. 'I've been having these panic attacks. Believe it or not, when I'm on my own, I break out into a sweat when I hear the slightest noise. It's really spoiled my life. I can't even sleep properly without taking tablets. I've decided to do something about it. You know Gwenda, the lady with the green dress, well she has a friend who had similar problems who went to this class. After four sessions, she said she became a different person.'

'Yes, but things like that don't bother me at all,' said Grindal.

'But it's not just for people who are afraid of being alone, it's for anyone who has emotional problems. It's called Emotional Management for Mature Adults.'

Grindal rolled his eyes upwards. 'But Moira, surely you don't expect me to go to something like that. Alright, I agree I might have a problem. But Classes. Do you really think I'm the type of person who would join in on one of those group therapy things? No, I don't think so.'

Moira was suddenly serious. 'Look, Grindal, I'll be honest with you. The main reason I'm asking you to go with me is because I'm afraid to go there by myself.'

'Then why bother?' said Grindal.

'You don't understand, it's not the class I'm afraid of, it's actually going there and coming back by myself. It's a night-time course which means I have to travel on the bus for half an hour each way. You know what it's like on the buses at night. All those young thugs and drug addicts.'

'I'm sure you would be alright,' said Grindal.

'Please, just for the first session. I'll pay for everything.'

'It's not that,' said Grindal. 'It's just that...'

He looked at Moira. The expression on her face was pleading with him to accept her request. He wondered for a moment if she might be using the fear tactic as a ploy just to get him to the class. He dismissed the idea. Not for any reason other than he did not wish to contemplate such a question.

'All right, but only for the first session,' he conceded.

Moira's face lit up like a beacon. 'Thank you, you're really kind.' She bent across and kissed him on the cheek.

Grindal was more circumspect. He pondered for a moment what he might have let himself in for. The feeling he had been conned crossed his mind, but he let it pass. *Maybe I might even get something out of it. Or more likely it will be a disaster.* The vision of sitting with a group of senile individuals and revealing his own shortcomings did not appeal to him. But Grindal knew he had a problem. Something had to be done about it. He made a promise to himself that he would try his very best to do what was asked of him, at least at the first class. After all, that was the only commitment he had made to Moira. If it turned out to be a useless exercise, then he would pull out of it. Moira would have to take a taxi.

As the thought occurred to him, Grindal wondered why she didn't take a taxi anyway.

'Can I get you another drink?' asked Moira, interrupting his line of thought.

'Yes please,' said Grindal. He gave her his empty glass and watched as she disappeared into the kitchen. Grindal could not help but notice that she was an attractive looking woman. As soon as the thought came to him, it was followed by the same niggling feelings of guilt he had experienced before.

Grindal looked around the room as he waited for Moira to return with his drink. The furnishings looked expensive, as did the large Persian rug which covered the polished timber floor. There were several strings of crystals which hung from the ceiling. They seemed to be placed randomly, yet for some reason did not look out of place as they sparkled in the subdued light. Grindal wondered if they served any purpose or whether they were purely for decoration.

An elderly woman in a bright green dress, came and sat on the sofa next to Grindal. He had been introduced to her earlier but as usual could not recall her name.

'Hello Grindal,' she said. 'Are you enjoying yourself'?

'Yes, thank you.'

'I'm just about to leave,' said the woman. 'I have a message for you, I meant to talk to you earlier, but you know how easy it is to get caught up in conversation.'

'A message,' said Grindal. He was quite curious what message could this woman have to give him. He had never seen her before in his life.

'Jessie says that you should stop worrying about things that don't really matter. She is very happy where she is. She says you must try and find happiness through the people around you. Life goes on. You shouldn't dwell on the past. Live for today and make some new memories.'

Grindal's mouth fell open. He tried to say something, but no words came out. He just looked at the woman before him still unable to believe what he had just heard.

'I'm going now,' she said. 'Perhaps we shall meet some other time.'

With that, she smiled and walked away. Grindal watched as she disappeared through the doorway.

'Please, wait.' He called out after her, but it was too late, she was gone.

Grindal watched as the woman disappeared through the doorway which led to the entry. His first reaction was to run after her. But he stopped himself, not wanting to look foolish. Perhaps it was some kind of sick joke, he thought. But how could anyone know. The words she used were exactly as Jessie would have said them.

'What's the matter with you? You look as if you've

seen a ghost.'

Grindal looked up to see Moira standing before him holding the drink she had fetched. He stared at her for a moment without replying. Still, absorbed in what he had just heard. 'Who was that woman?' he asked.

'What woman?' replied Moira.

'The one in the green dress and the bracelets,' replied Grindal.

'Oh, the one who just left. That's Gwenda, Gwenda Ross. Why do you ask?'

'Did you tell her anything about me?'

'No, why should I do that?'

Grindal looked at Moira, studying her reaction to see if he could determine any flicker of deception in her expression. His mind would not allow him to believe that anyone could say the things the woman had said to him, without some kind of prior knowledge. But there was nothing. Only a look of concern that someone may have upset him.

'Is there something wrong?' asked Moira.

'No . . . She said my late wife had given her a message for me. It was really strange.'

'What . . . The message?'

'No, not the message.' Grindal looked at her

incredulously. 'You don't think it's a bit unusual for someone to give a message from a dead person to a complete stranger?'

'Not with Gwenda. She's a clairvoyant, she sees and hears things. Sometimes she can talk to the dead.'

Grindal shook his head. 'You don't expect me to believe that, do you?'

'What you believe, is up to you,' said Moira. 'Did the message make any sense?'

'Yes,' replied Grindal. 'That's the problem.' He was confused and still refused to take the information he had been given, on face value. His thoughts darted from one scenario to another, trying to make some sense out of the communication he had been given. He even contemplated that Gwenda Ross might be a member of The Brotherhood of The Second Coming. A plant sent by Brother James who could have been given inside information by Clare. Grindal realised the confusion was quickly leading him into paranoia. Nevertheless, he determined he would broach the subject with Clare in any case.

'Do you want to talk about it?' asked Moira.

'No, I prefer not to,' replied Grindal.

'Come on,' said Moira. 'Enough of this despondency, let's go and see what Egor is up to. Last time I saw him he was doing his impression of James Cagney holding up a bank.' She took Grindal by the arm and eased him out of the sofa. He was not really interested in what Egor was doing, but some kind of diversion might be a good thing.

Grindal was still totally preoccupied with what Gwenda Ross had said to him and no matter how hard he tried; the message kept coming back.

The rest of the evening went by without incident. A rousing chorus of "Happy Birthday" was followed by a smorgasbord which would have put many restaurants to shame. Grindal, was now more relaxed, probably due to the amount of alcohol he had consumed, rather than any mental calmness on his part. He surprised himself, by actually making conversation with the people around him. The fact was he was enjoying himself but would never admit it.

Soon people started to leave. The clock on the wall said eleven fifty. Grindal looked at it and then at his own wristwatch as if to confirm to himself that it was time he too should be leaving. He watched as Moira bid goodbye to her guests. She seemed to be happy and he was glad he had not spoiled the occasion by arguing with any of the guests. He whispered to himself. 'Well at least Clare will be pleased.' But most of all he remembered about Gwenda Ross and the message she had given him from Jessie.

CHAPTER 8

When Grindal returned home, the house was dark. Thankfully the Brotherhood was long gone. He crept into the bedroom not wanting to disturb Josh who from the sound of his deep breathing, was fast asleep. It was a long time before sleep enveloped him. The vision of Gwenda Ross giving her message would not leave.

The next morning, he was tired and decided to stay in bed until everyone had left the house. It was raining outside which prevented him from taking his usual walk to the local newsagent for the morning paper. Instead he listened to the talk back show on the local radio station. The Minister for Social Services was taking calls from pensioners. He was trying desperately to convince them of his genuine concern for their problems. Grindal listened to his replies to their questions and repeatedly interjected with cries of 'bullshit' and 'rubbish.' After ten minutes, he turned the radio off in disgust.

The rest of the day he spent pacing around the house like a caged animal. He had lost the art of relaxing many months ago. His mind would not be quiet, it jumped around reviewing and remembering countless events from past and present. By late afternoon he was tired and agitated. He resolved that weather permitting he would not hang around the house the next day. He would go out. Where to, he was not sure, but he would go somewhere.

When Clare and Kate returned from school, Grindal was persuaded by Kate to go to the park with Bruce. Grindal was not really thrilled with the idea but found any request from his granddaughter hard to refuse. He also reasoned that he had not been out all day and the fresh air would do him good.

Bruce, as usual was on his best behavior as they walked to the local park. The rain had stopped along with the wind which had been blowing all day. Grindal and Kate sat on the bench watching Bruce chase the seagulls which congregated near a small artificial lake.

'Did you have a good time at the birthday party Grandad?' asked Kate.

'Yes, as a matter of fact I did,' replied Grindal.

'What was your night like with Mum's friends?'

'Well, it was sort of alright, but everyone is really serious. Brother James is really strict; he tells everyone what to do.'

Grindal did not pursue the matter. He couldn't imagine Brother James telling him what to do.

'Did Moira get lots of birthday presents?' asked Kate.

'Yes, quite a few.'

'What were they?'

'Well, let me see, there were some books, some bottles of wine, and of course flowers and chocolates.'

'Did she like your present?'

'Yes, she thought the flowers were beautiful and the chocolates were her favorite kind. They played nice music. The sort of olden day stuff that people grandad's age like. And guess what?'

'What.'

'Moira gave me a really large piece of birthday cake for you and Mum.'

'Oh goody, I can't wait. Can we eat it after dinner?'

'If Mum says, it's ok, then why not.'

Grindal watched the happy expression on his granddaughter's face and realised he cared for her a great deal. They sat in silence for a while, watching Bruce, who was now sitting on the grass beside the bench.

'I told my friend at school about you today, and she said that Grindal is a funny name, I told her she shouldn't be rude,' she added.

'I hope you didn't argue,' said Grindal.

'Well sort of, but not really,' replied Kate.

'I suppose it is a funny name when you think of it. I've never met any other Grindal's. Have you?'

Kate laughed. 'No.'

'It means green valley, it's a Welsh name. My grandmother was Welsh, and I think she was the one who suggested it,' said Grindal.

'I'll tell her that tomorrow,' said Kate.

'Time to get back I think,' said Grindal. 'Mum will have dinner ready.'

'And after dinner, there's birthday cake,' laughed Kate.

They walked slowly back to the house. The fresh air had cleared Grindal's head. He was now feeling much better.

That evening, everybody was in good spirits. Even Josh stayed home and after dinner everyone sat in the lounge room and watched television. When Josh was home there was a particular routine. Grindal waited for Josh to go to bed and then waited at least an hour before he followed. This allowed Josh some privacy to get settled in for the night. Up until now the routine had worked out well. Grindal hoped it would stay that way. There was an unwritten agreement between the two males. They each gave the other privacy where possible. They never talked to each other in the bedroom, not even to say good morning. Josh was still very distant from Grindal, but Grindal reasoned that the distance was not getting any greater and for the time being he was happy to settle for that.

As Grindal lay awake in bed that night, he remembered his promise to himself that he would go out somewhere the next day. But as much as he tried, he could not think of anywhere that interested him. After a while he stopped worrying about it.

The next morning, he resigned himself to staying home all day. At least it wasn't raining, and he was able to fetch his newspaper. Just as he walked into the front garden, he bumped into Moira, who by the way she was dressed, was obviously going out.

'Morning Grindal. Nice day, isn't it?'

'Yes, it is,' replied Grindal. 'Going out for the day, are you?' he asked.

'Not really for the day, just a couple of hours at the bowling club. A bit of a meeting with the ladies auxiliary committee. What are you up to today?'

'Oh, nothing much. Probably go for a walk later,' Grindal replied.

'Would you like to come with me?' asked Moira. 'There's nothing much going on, but maybe we can have a bit of lunch at the club when my meeting is finished?'

Grindal did not need to be asked twice. Anything was

better than staying home all day with Bruce and the television. 'Can you give me a minute to get changed?'

Fifteen minutes later they were sitting on the bus, heading for the bowling club. Grindal was pleased with his unexpected opportunity for a day out. He and Moira chatted about nothing in particular for the short time it took to get to the bowling club.

The bus dropped them virtually right outside the door. Moira walked quickly she was worried that already she was ten minutes late for her meeting. They had previously agreed that for the hour it would take Moira to finish her meeting, Grindal would find a comfortable corner and read his newspaper. After that they would have some lunch.

When Moira pushed through the large glass swing door, they were confronted by a tall gaunt looking man in his late sixties. He was dressed immaculately in his cream bowling regalia. He stared suspiciously at Grindal. The gaze was made even more piercing by the fact that he was at least a foot taller. Grindal refused to be intimidated and stared straight back at the man without blinking.

'Good morning Basil,' said Moira.

'Good morning Moira. I see we have a friend with us today.'

Basil inspected Grindal from head to toe, much like an

157

officer inspecting one of the ranks.

'Yes, this is Grindal, Grindal Falcon. Grindal is a good friend of mine. He's the one that saved me from the burglar,' said Moira proudly. 'Grindal, this is Basil, Basil Fielding. Basil is our Club Secretary,' said Moira introducing the two men.

'Quite the hero,' said Basil. 'The way Moira described you, I thought you would be much taller. Still, it's amazing what people can do when confronted by an emergency. Well done.'

The answer was given with the faintest hint of disdain. Grindal was quick to pick up the taint of jealousy in Basil's demeanor. *Could it be that big Basil has his eye on Moira?*

Basil held out his hand. Grindal took it. As the two hands joined, the simple handshake turned into a contest about who had the strongest grip. For the few short seconds of the exchange the two men smiled at each other, neither wishing to show any discomfort. Basil's hand was much larger than Grindal's and for that reason Grindal lost. When the contest finished Grindal came away with a sore hand and a dented ego. Basil was beaming, he knew he had won. He condescendingly patted Grindal on the shoulder.

'Welcome to the club,' said Basil.

Moira in the meantime had not noticed that anything

unusual had passed between the two men. She was busily sorting through a bunch of papers relating to her meeting.

'Can you look after Grindal for me whilst I'm in the meeting Basil?' asked Moira. 'I'm sure you two have a lot in common. Basil was a pilot in the last war, he won a medal for bravery,' she added.

'I'm sure Grindal doesn't want to hear about my exploits,' said Basil. 'Perhaps he can tell me about some of his. I'm sure a brave chap like him will have lots of them.'

The eyes of the two men met each other in a brief stare. The contest was still on.

When the formalities of signing in as a visitor were concluded, Grindal followed Moira into the Members Lounge. Fortunately, Basil stayed in the foyer, having been interrupted by some club business. Grindal hoped that he would stay away but knew in his heart that Basil would be back to resume the contest.

Grindal watched as Moira disappeared into the committee room. He bought himself a cup of coffee at the bar and then positioned himself at the far side of the room on a small table. From where he sat, he could survey the whole room. There was no one sitting on the tables around him which made Grindal feel relatively secure. People from various tables turned to stare at him occasionally. No doubt he was the subject of much gossip among the small groups that were clustered around the room.

Grindal studied the people in the room. Most were dressed in bowling uniform but those that were not seemed to be rather formerly attired. The men in jackets and ties and the woman dressed more as if they were going to church, not to a social club.

Grindal himself was wearing an open necked shirt and a pair of jeans. *Obviously, Basil was not impressed with my attire.* He decided to ignore the stares he was getting and concentrate on his newspaper. Only five minutes passed before he was interrupted.

'Can I get you a drink of something?' asked Basil. 'Maybe a pint of beer?'

Grindal ignored what was obviously meant to be an insult and carried on reading his paper. Basil sat on the chair opposite him. Grindal did not look up.

'Have you known Moira long?' asked Basil.

'No.'

'We've been friends for some time. We're really quite close,' said Basil.

'Really,' accentuated Grindal. 'I didn't see you at her birthday party the other night.'

'Yes, well, I had something on that night otherwise I

would have been there.'

Basil was hesitant in his reply which brought Grindal to the conclusion that possibly he wasn't invited. Grindal buried himself in his newspaper in the hope that Basil would take the hint and leave. Basil began tapping his fingers on the table. The tapping seemed to be getting louder as the seconds passed. Grindal looked up.

'Do you mind,' he said. 'I'm trying to concentrate on my newspaper.'

'Sorry,' said Basil. 'It's a bit of a nervous habit I picked up in the war. Were you in the war?' The force with which the question was asked demanded an answer.

'Which war was that?' replied Grindal, determined not to play the game.

'W.W. Two of course, the big one.' Basil waited for his reply. As the seconds passed, the look of confidence returned to his face.

'It was a long time ago, I don't remember', said Grindal.

'Don't remember, what do you mean you don't remember?' Basil was becoming frustrated with the evasive replies he was getting.

'Alright, if I tell you what I did, will you promise not to tell anyone?' said Grindal.

'Yes, of course,' replied Basil, who now had a look of anticipation on his face.

Grindal motioned Basil to come nearer. He then leaned over and whispered in his ear. 'I was a Bugler in the Secret Service.'

It took Basil a few seconds to realise he had been outmaneuvered. When he did, he was not very happy.

'Really, some people have no respect,' he spluttered. With that, he stormed off towards the bar muttering to himself.

Grindal watched him go. 'Up yours Basil,' he said to himself.

He looked at his wristwatch. He had only been in the club for half an hour and already had made an enemy of the club secretary. But he reasoned to himself that there was no real harm done just a bit of dented pride on both sides. Hopefully that would be the end of the matter. He would have his lunch with Moira and with any luck never come to the bowling club again. He looked across at Basil who was standing at the bar with a group of his cronies. There were lots of stares coming his way. Grindal returned the stares and moved his chair around so that he had his back to them. Then with some mental effort on his part focused his attention back on his newspaper.

'Moira should be finished soon, and then you'll be able to leave.'

Grindal looked up. He couldn't believe it. Basil was back. He seated himself at the table. Grindal took a deep breath. He closed the newspaper, sat back in his chair, folded his arms and looked across at Basil.

'What do you want? Haven't you got lots of Secretary things to do?' asked Grindal.

'Not really,' said Basil. 'It seems we got off on the wrong foot. I just thought we might have a bit of a chat. Sort of make things friendly again if you know what I mean.'

Grindal didn't believe a word of it but decided to play the game to see where it was leading. He didn't speak but waited for Basil to begin what he thought might be, some kind of interrogation.

'Do you bowl?' asked Basil.'

'No,' replied Grindal.

There was a few seconds delay before Basil asked his next question.

'Been retired long?'

'Long enough.'

'I was in banking myself, before I retired. What did you do?' asked Basil.

'Is it any of your business?' Grindal was becoming

163

annoyed with the prying questions.

'Just a simple question, old chap, no need to get annoyed.'

'All right, I'll tell you, just to get you off my back,' said Grindal. 'If you must know, I've just come out of prison. I've been there for the last fourteen years.'

Basil was visibly shocked.

'What . . . er what was it. What was it you were in for?' His fingers that had been drumming on the table stopped as he waited for the reply.

Grindal screwed up his face and stared directly into Basil's eyes. 'Murder.'

'Murder! What . . . er... who... who did you murder?' Basil's face was white.

Grindal was beginning to enjoy himself. He contorted his face into a mad looking expression and began to twitch his eye.

'The doctor told me not to talk about it, it sets me off.' He twitched his eye more rapidly.

'Sets you off,' said Basil, who was now looking very alarmed. He was not sure what this madman might do next.

Grindal relaxed his contorted features. 'It's alright Basil, I took my pills this morning.' Basil got up, now in a hurry to leave. Grindal caught hold of his arm and pulled him back into his chair. 'It wasn't really my fault,' said Grindal rolling his eyes. 'It was just that he annoyed me so much. I couldn't help myself. He was simply unlucky I had the axe in my hand. The next thing I knew, I'd chopped him to pieces. You must remember it. There was a lot of publicity at the time. The axe man from Altona. That was me.' Grindal smiled at Basil and let go of his arm.

Basil couldn't leave fast enough. He backed away from the table. 'But you've taken your pills today? You're alright now?'

Grindal sat back in his chair.

'Couldn't be better.'

He watched as Basil retreated back to the bar. He was feeling quite pleased with himself. Basil had actually believed everything he said. 'Stupid arshole.' He mouthed the words whilst looking in the direction of the bar. Basil was now surrounded by a group of men and woman who were all staring at Grindal. They seemed to be involved in a heated discussion. One of the men in the group was pointing at Grindal and at the same time pushing Basil in his direction. Basil appeared to be reluctant, but it seemed the group were insisting.

Grindal watched with interest. Eventually Basil slowly approached him. Grindal twitched his eye and contorted his face into the mad expression he had assumed earlier. He then relaxed and smiled. Basil was hesitant and uncertain.

'Any problem's Basil?' he asked.

'No, not really, it's just that the committee thinks it might be better if you leave. We . . . er... don't allow ex-convicts in the club. You understand, it's one of those rules they all feel strongly about.'

Grindal motioned Basil to come closer. When he was close enough Grindal leaned over and whispered in his ear. 'If you don't fuck off, I'll find out where you live and burn your house down.'

Basil was aghast. 'You what!' He took a quick jump backwards. There was a chair directly behind him which had been pulled out from an adjacent table. He hit the chair with the back of his leg. Unfortunately, the chair was wedged against the side of the table. Basil's legs stopped whilst the rest of his body kept going.

Grindal watched in amazement as Basil flew backwards, arms spread-eagled crashing flat on his back across the table. What made matters worse was the fact that the table was full of empty glasses. These flew in all directions smashing noisily onto the tiled floor.

'Assault, assault. Stop him he's a murderer,' screamed Basil as he rolled around in the broken glass trying to stand up.

Grindal put his hands on his hips and laughed out loud. 'Get up, you stupid arse. I never touched you.'

'Someone help me,' shouted Basil. 'He's a maniac. Call the police.'

Grindal was still laughing. He thought it especially funny when Basil cut his hand on the broken glass and then wiped his face. It made him look as if he had been in a real fight.

'Serves you right anyway. Nosy bastard,' he shouted at Basil who was still trying to haul himself to his feet.

Grindal's laughter did not last long. Within a few seconds he was pounced on from behind. Lots of hands and arms seemed to wrap themselves around him. Someone grabbed his legs. It was now Grindal's turn to be on the floor. As much as he cursed and struggled, he was soon held fast Even though most of his attackers were sixty or seventy years old, their combined weight was too much for Grindal. They were all puffing and panting.

'Get him. Hold him. Ring the police.'

Through a small gap in the pile of bodies on top of him Grindal spied Basil hovering above him. He could not protect himself as he saw the big fist coming towards his face. The blow hit him square in the eye.

'I'll kill you. You bastard,' he shouted.

But this only made matters worse. The murderer was now threatening to strike again. Everyone heard the threat.

When the police finally arrived Grindal, was allowed to stand up. His first mistake was to take a swing at Basil who was telling everyone how Grindal attacked him when he was asked to leave. The police officers, who, had never seen a pensioner's brawl before, decided that he would play it safe and handcuff the main troublemaker.

Grindal was unceremoniously cuffed and led outside to be locked in the police car while statements were taken. At the door, he was confronted by Moira. She was crying profusely.

'Oh Grindal, how could you. How could you do this to me? Attacking one of my best friends. Poor Basil, you might have killed him.'

'Poor Basil. I'll give him poor Basil when I lay my hands on him.'

'Oh, you beast, I never want to see you again, ever.' Moira burst into another bout of tears.

The last Grindal saw of her she was being consoled by her friends.

'Come along sir, just calm down. I think you're in enough trouble as it is,' said the police officer.

'I never laid a glove on him. Honest.' But as much as Grindal protested, it seemed that no one was interested in his side of the story.

'You just sit in there and keep quiet,' said the police officer.

With his hands handcuffed behind his back Grindal did not have any option but to do as he was told. His eye was throbbing where he had been struck by Basil, and he had a big headache to match.

He sat in the police car for what seemed like hours. Eventually the two police officers came out of the club and jumped into the car.

'I think you had better come down to the station and answer some questions,' said one of them. 'It seems that some people in there think you might be some kind of maniacal axe murderer. I doubt it myself,' he smirked. 'But then that bloke you attacked in there is a close friend of my Sargent.'

'Looks like it's not your day, old man,' added the other officer.

Grindal did not reply. His arms were aching from the handcuffs and his head now felt as if it was ready to explode.

'Can you take these things off my hands?' he asked. 'I'm in a lot of pain.'

'Oh, we couldn't do that, now could we. You might attack us and steal the car.'

Both of the policemen in the car laughed.

Grindal did not appreciate the two men having a laugh at his expense. 'Yes, I can see an old man might be a bit too much for a couple of fairies like you,' he said quietly.
The man sitting in the back seat with him was not amused. He grabbed Grindal by the hair and stuck his thumb into the bruised eye. Grindal let out a sharp cry. The pain was like an electric shock.

'You're a real glutton for punishment, aren't you?'

'Lay off Bob,' said the driver. He's just a stupid old cunt that's had too much to drink.'

Grindal caught the look on the driver's face. It showed concern and alarm.

After that, nothing else was spoken in the car. Within a few minutes they arrived at the police station.

The handcuffs were removed, and he was taken to an interview room. The driver of the car and another police officer questioned him for about fifteen minutes. It soon became clear to them that there would be no points scored by charging Grindal with anything. He was not the hardened criminal they thought they might have picked up. The interview came to a very swift conclusion when Grindal mentioned he had been assaulted in the police car by one of the officers.

The two interviewing officers left the room. Within five minutes they returned.

'You can go now, Mr. Falcon. If we need you, we'll be in touch.'

'I bet you will,' said Grindal.

He knew he might cause a lot of problems for them if he pursued the assault claim. *An old man with no previous record being assaulted by police. The newspapers would love it.*

He also knew that he was tired and, in some pain, and that the police had contacted Clare at her work. Who knows what they had told her? All he wanted now was to get home. What started out as a quiet lunch date had turned into a nightmare. The worst thing was that he had not been the instigator of any of it. At least, that's how he saw it.

When he walked out of the police station Grindal was in a real mess. His shirt and trousers were torn, his eye was swollen and there was blood on the side of his face. To add to that he was feeling dizzy.

He walked up the street to a phone box and called a taxi. When the cab arrived, the driver looked suspiciously at Grindal.

'Shit mate, what happened to you?' asked the driver.

'You should have seen the other bloke,' Grindal replied.

His attempt at humour belied the fact that he was almost ready to pass out. When he finally reached home it was all he could do to open the door and stagger into his room.

******

CHAPTER 9

W hen Clare arrived home and found her father collapsed on the bed with torn cloths and blood smeared face, she thought he was dead. The call from the police station had already alarmed her, but they had not mentioned he had been injured. They had only asked her questions regarding his identity. All they would say was, that he was helping them with their enquiries. She immediately called an ambulance and Grindal was rushed off to hospital.

The next recollection of the event for Grindal, was when he woke up in the emergency ward. Luckily there was no permanent injury. He was merely suffering from concussion. Nevertheless, he was kept in the ward overnight and allowed to leave the next morning.

All the time this had been happening, Clare had been very patient. She had not asked him the full story of what had happened. Grindal had promised he would explain when he was feeling better. This he did the following day.

To his surprise Clare was very supportive. She did not berate him but instead severely criticized Moira, the police and the person called Basil. Within half an hour of his telling the story, she had talked to all of them.

Ignoring Grindal's protestations, she firstly called the police station and made a formal complaint to the desk Sargent. This included possible assault, and not giving medical aid to an obviously injured person. She was immediately transferred to an Inspector Reece who said he would follow up the matter without delay. Her next telephone call was to the Bowling Club. She asked for the Secretary, and when Basil answered the phone, she managed to give him a short tirade of invective before he hung up.

Grindal could not believe that his daughter was capable of such vehemence. Whilst she never used any foul language, her tone of voice was powerful and intimidating. When the call was terminated, she put the phone down hard and without further comment went straight next door to see Moira. Grindal walked to the open front door. If he looked through at an acute angle, he could just see across to the house next door. When Moira answered the door, Grindal could not hear what was being said although he could discern raised voices. After two or three minutes, he recognized the now somewhat familiar sound of Moira bursting into tears.

When Clare returned, she was breathing hard and muttering to herself.

'Now you just sit down and stay out of trouble.' She pointed her finger at Grindal.

He decided to do as he was told. He had not seen this side of his daughter before. He had always regarded her as being submissive and withdrawn. This was something new and he was very proud of her. For the first time Grindal could remember, decisions which directly affected him and over which he had control, were being made by someone else. He felt almost a sense of relief.

******

The next few days Grindal spent quietly recuperating from his recent adventure. Clare, Kate and even Josh had rallied around him giving him support and sympathy. The episode had created a bonding which had not been between them before. Once or twice whilst going for his newspaper he had noticed Moira peering from behind her curtains, but there had been no other contact. His eye was not bothering him now even though it was still quite black.

It was a Tuesday morning and the sun was shining even though it was still cold. As Grindal was returning from his daily foray to the newsagent, he noticed a large van parked outside what had been an empty house across the road from Clare's place. On the pavement standing next to the van was a woman who was trying to negotiate a large table through the front gate. She was dressed in blue denim bib and brace overalls and was wearing a colored head scarf which tied up her hair. She stopped her struggle when Grindal passed and looked him straight in the eye. Her smile was quite disarming.

'Hello, my name is Tulip. Will you help me with this table? It doesn't seem to want to fit through the gate.'

Grindal wedged his newspaper into the palings of the fence.

'Ok.'

Between the two of them lifting the table was easy. Within a few seconds it was over the fence and inside the house.

The first thing that came to Grindal's attention when they entered the house was the loud music coming from the room at the bottom of the hallway.

'I hope you like Bob Dylan,' said Tulip raising her voice above the vibrating sound. Two voices could be heard accompanying the music; one in tune and the other way off of key. They quickly moved the table into one of the rooms. There were books all over the floor along with a desk, which was much too large for the small room. The addition of the table made it even more crowded.

'That's great,' said Tulip. 'Thanks very much.' She

stared for a few seconds at the mess in the room. 'I must introduce you to my husband; he's the one, making all the noise down the passage. Hang on a minute; I'll see if I can get him to turn down that racket.'

'Time for a break Garth,' she shouted as she left the room.

Grindal was suddenly on his own. He looked around the room wondering for a moment what he was doing there. The walls were filled with framed Diplomas and Degrees from various educational institutions. Grindal looked more closely. Garth Bender, who was presumably Tulip's husband, was definitely no slouch. He had a PhD. In Psychology a Degree in Philosophy and another one in Law.

'Don't take any notice of them. I only hang them up to remind me how many years of my life I wasted before I finally had the courage to leave school.'

A well-rounded figure in his early fifties walked slowly into the room. Again, Grindal was taken with the warm smile that was offered as the words were spoken.

'Hello, I'm Garth. Tulip tells me you're helping us to move in.'

Grindal could not help but smile back. 'It looks as if I am. I'm Grindal Falcon, pleased to meet you.'

'What an excellent name,' said Garth.

177

'You think so? Most people think Grindal is a bit strange.

'No not Grindal, that's very strange, nearly as bad as Bender.

'Falcon,' said Garth intensely. 'It sounds sleek. I shall call you Falcon.'

Grindal stared at Garth incredulously. He was wearing a genuine smile that could not be argued with.

'Then he shall call you Bender,' said Tulip as she pushed passed her husband. 'Let's have some coffee before you scare off our new neighbor. At least I think he's a neighbor?' She looked in askance at Grindal.

'Yes, I live across the road.'

The three of them then retired to the kitchen which was in a big a mess as was the rest of the house. Tulips scrambled around among the pots and pans and finally found three mugs.

'Have you lived here long?' asked Tulip.

'No, not long at all. My house burned down. After a few failed attempts to live elsewhere, I eventually ended up living with my daughter.'

'You don't sound too happy about it. Is it that bad?' asked Garth.

'Don't be nosy Garth, we've only just met Grindal and

you're asking him his life story,' said Tulip.

'Don't worry, that's all right. Clare, my daughter is really good to me. It's just that since my wife died, I've found it a bit difficult to adjust. I always seem to stuff up anything I get involved in,' said Grindal with a grimace.

'Well, you're in good company here Falcon. When it comes to stuff ups, Tulip and I are professionals. The thing is, we don't give a family fuck about anything. You should try it some time,' laughed Garth.

Grindal smiled, he was feeling quite relaxed with this pair of strangers. The lay back attitude they had seemed to be contagious.

'Are you a teacher?' asked Grindal.

'Many years ago, I used to lecture in philosophy. Eventually I decided to practice what I was preaching. Tulip and I are what is commonly known as dropouts. We are totally selfish; we live life the way most people can only dream of.

The trick is, to eliminate all the garbage that's been pushed down your throat ever since you were born. The more you eliminate, the fewer worries you have. The fewer worries you have, the more life is worth living. In a nutshell, we are mentally and spiritually successful. The fact that we are socially and financially total failures, adds to our success. We have our books, we have Bob Dylan, and we have each other. What more is there in life.'

Grindal was not surprised when Garth took out a pouch and rolled himself what Grindal guessed and later on confirmed, was a large joint of marihuana.

'Would you like a snort of weed, Falcon?'

'No thanks, I gave it up in the sixties.'

'Good for you Falcon, I admire a man with will power.'

'Do you take sugar in your caffeine?' asked Tulip.

'White with no sugar'

Grindal spent the rest of the day with Garth and Tulip Bender. He could not remember when he had enjoyed such good company. They had homemade bread rolls with cheese and salad for lunch. Garth treated Grindal to a special selection of Bob Dylan records from his large collection and by the end of the day turned him into a fan.

It was four in the afternoon when Grindal eventually went home. Clare noticed his happy disposition, especially when he had a good word and a pat on the head for Bruce.

'My, you're in a good mood you must have been somewhere special today?'

'Yes, I have,' replied Grindal.

He then proceeded to tell her of the day he had spent

with the new neighbors. He got a little bit carried away and let it slip that Garth smoked marihuana. This of course made Clare worried that he had got mixed up with a pair of drug addicts. No matter how Grindal tried to explain to her about the Benders'' he couldn't quite convince her that they were a wonderful couple. Josh on the other hand seemed very interested, for some reason. He even dug out an old Bob Dylan record which Grindal inspected to see if any of his now favorite songs were on it.

The only thing that spoiled the evening was when Clare reminded him of his promise to attend the next meeting of The Brotherhood of the Second Coming. It was something he was not looking forward to. But he had made a promise and felt that he owed it to Clare to at least attend one meeting. The thought occurred to him that Garth might have some ideas of how he might handle the situation.

Grindal had been given an open invitation to call in on the Bender's any time. He thought he might call in the following day to help Garth move some of the furniture into place. Grindal felt good about going, more especially because he had learned that Tulip had a back injury and was not supposed to lift anything.

The next morning Grindal stuck to his routine as if to convince himself that calling on the Bender's had no special significance. He returned slowly from the newsagent reading the headlines and skimming the first few pages as he walked. When he arrived at the front door, it was ajar. He knocked tentatively.

'Come in, whoever you are,' Tulip shouted from inside.

Grindal walked down the passageway into the house. As he passed the room which Grindal presumed was the office, he saw Garth collating a large bundle of papers. He looked up as Grindal stood in the doorway.

'Morning Falcon. How are you today?'

'Good, thanks. What are you up to?'

'Nothing much. Just finishing an article, I'm doing for the 'Current Affairs Bulletin.'

'What's that about, politics?'

'No, just some boring thing about the ethics of genetic engineering. A pain in the arse really, but it does help to pay the rent.'

'Is that what you do for a living, write stuff for magazines?'

'Yes. It's the only thing I'm capable of doing that doesn't require me to answer to anyone. Anyway, I'll be finished in a minute, go and have a coffee with Tulip, and warm up the record player,' he laughed.

Grindal took the hint and went into the kitchen. Tulip

was on the top of a step ladder attempting to put some boxes into one of the cupboards. The stepladder was about a foot too short and she was not having much success.

'Looks like a job for someone about five feet ten inches tall?'

'Or someone my size with a bigger step ladder,' she replied.

Grindal changed places with Tulip, and under her directions had everything stored away within a few minutes. Sounds of Bob Dylan came from the other end of the house.

It sounds like Garth's finished his article,' said Tulip.

A few seconds later a smiling Garth entered the kitchen singing and swaying to the music in the background.

Both Tulip and Grindal cringed at the off- key sounds coming from the rotund figure.

'All finished, so I think I'll take the rest of the day off,' he smiled.

'It's a hard life you lead. Just sit down and relax while I make you some coffee,' said Tulip.

Garth sat at the table and proceeded to roll himself a joint.

'Are you sure you won't have one Falcon? It'll do you the world of good.'

Grindal declined. He sat in silence as Tulip and Garth

discussed the article he had just completed. It was a bit over his head, but the opinions Garth expressed seemed to make sense.

Tulip served the coffee. 'Enough of this highbrow stuff; we'll frighten our guest away, never to return.'

'No, nothing of the sort, it's really quite interesting,' said Grindal.

'Anyway Falcon, what have you been up to? Not stuffing anything up I hope?'

'Not yet, but I've got the perfect opportunity coming up very soon.'

'Sounds interesting, tell me more,' said Garth.

'Well, its Clare, my daughter, remember I told you that she's involved with this religious mob.'

Both Tulip and Garth nodded in assent.

'Well, I promised that I would sit in on their next meeting at the house. The trouble is, I've got this thing about religion. As soon as anyone starts pushing their line, I can't help myself. I open my mouth and tell them what I think. Clare would be devastated, and I don't want that. But I just know it's going to happen.'

Garth took a sip on his coffee and a long drag on his joint. 'You know your trouble Falcon? You resent other people's opinions.'

Grindal was surprised at the comment, but as it was said with a smile, it did not bother him.

'What do you mean?'

'Socrates explained it quite simply. People have no right to force their beliefs and opinions on others. But by the same token, you have no right to force your beliefs and opinions on them. The positive things in life such as love, kindness, compassion, are the same for everyone no matter what they believe in. People should be encouraged to pursue what they believe in their own way. The fact that you get upset when people express an opinion which you believe to be false shows a lack of confidence in your own viewpoint.'

Grindal reflected for a few moments on what Garth said.

'But the bloke that runs the show is a real puritan who thinks he knows it all,' protested Grindal.

'You mean, he believes he is one of the trusted guardians to the gates of heaven? Undeserving troublemakers such as your good self will not get a look in unless they are prepared to grovel to the keeper.'

'That's exactly right,' said Grindal. 'And I'm dam sure I'm not going to brown-nose to a prick like Brother James. Excuse the language Tulip.'

'Oh, don't you worry about that Brother Grindal, just

get it off your chest,' she laughed.

'Well Falcon, instead of getting all shitty, why not respond with some logical argument that supports your point of view,' offered Garth.

'I don't know about that. I doubt if I'd be able to hold a logical conversation with someone like Brother James.'

'Well in that case Falcon your fucked. You'll just have to sit there and smile. A few hallelujahs and praise the lord, and everyone will think you're a great bloke. No need to believe anything that's said, no need to upset anyone. What do you think?'

Garth smiled and took another long drag on his joint.

'You're not religious, are you?' asked Grindal with some hesitation.

'You mean, do I believe in God?'

'I suppose so.'

'As a matter of fact, I tend to follow the same philosophy as Bronislaw Malinowski. He analyzed religion as an escape from the stress of powerlessness. Such as we might feel in the face of death. Tulip on the other hand is an Advaitist.

'A what?'

'It's the non-dualistic philosophy of Vedanta,' said Tulip.

'You've lost me,' said Grindal shaking his head.

'To put it simply, the Advaitists declare that if there is a God, then that God must be the material and efficient cause of the universe. Not only is God the creator, He is also the created. God himself is the universe. Thus, in fact we are all Gods, just as there is no difference between one drop of water and the whole ocean.'

Tulip smiled at the blank look on Grindal's face.

'That's a hell of a long way from Jesus and the loaves and fishes,' said Grindal.

'Very true,' said Garth. But that goes back to our original proposition, that people have the right to pursue what they believe in their own way.'

Grindal reflected for a moment. 'I'm sure your right, but that Brother James is still a miserable bastard.'

Garth laughed.

'That's enough philosophy for today, time for some more music. Perhaps as a refreshing change we shall have some Donovan. Do you like Donovan Falcon?'

'Is that classical?' asked Grindal.

'Yes, very classical,' replied Garth.

Grindal spent most of the day pottering around and generally helping out.

The Benders' had moved from a much larger residence

and found it difficult to fit all their belongings into the small house. The spare room was overflowing with books and files that had been disgorged from several tea-chests.

That evening Grindal tried to explain to Clare about Vedanta. It seemed to be going well until he got to the part where everyone was a God. Clare decided that the Benders' were at best misguided drug addicts who were trying to fill her father's head with sacrilegious lies. Grindal decided it might be better if he didn't mention the Bender's to Clare in future.

After dinner, he stepped outside for a breath of air. It was just on dusk and a few spots of rain were beginning to fall. As he was about to go back inside, he heard a car pull up at the front of Moira's house. Out of sheer curiosity he waited to see who the visitor might be. Standing in the shadow of the fence, he was able to watch unobserved. He recognised the tall gangly frame of Basil from the bowling club. He ambled down the driveway. He was wearing a big silly grin on his face. It took all Grindal's self-control not to jump out and confront him. Instead he watched silently as Basil was welcomed at the front door.

'Toffee nosed prick,' said Grindal under his breath.

He went back inside the house but was now agitated. He sat in an armchair and rubbed his still bruised eye as he contemplated his own irritation. As much as he tried Grindal was unable to concentrate on the television. After about an hour he decided to go outside for another breath of air. Clare did not notice the biro he picked up from the table on the way out.

As he reached the front gate a quick look up and down the street showed that no one was around. The ballpoint pen was the perfect instrument for what he had in mind. It took only five minutes to let down all four tires on Basil's car. Grindal went back inside feeling much better. Three hours later he laid in bed smiling as he heard the loud curses coming through the front bedroom window.

******

CHAPTER 10

Over the following days both by intention and desire, Grindal formed a strong friendship with the Benders'. They seemed to have very few friends of their own. Grindal guessed that this was because they lived life as they had done in the sixties. For some reason, they had never moved on. Nevertheless, Grindal liked them a lot. He enjoyed their company. To him they were straight forward and honest people who enjoyed life in their own way.

Grindal appreciated their tolerance of his own somewhat antiquated views on life. Garth had a way of explaining things that made some of Grindal's opinions seem totally illogical. Yet the way he did it, with a smile and a joke somehow made him appreciate the advice.

Grindal's daughter Clare still had deep concerns about his relationship with the Benders'. She considered them to be undesirable. And yet, she had recently made a comment over dinner that he had become less dogmatic. Grindal told her in good humor that maybe her prayers were being answered.

******

It was Thursday morning. As usual everyone was running late. Breakfast was consumed as quickly as possible. Clare, Josh and Kate busied themselves preparing for the day ahead. Grindal toyed with the eggs Clare had prepared for him and eventually decided he did not want them.

'What's wrong Dad?' asked Clare. 'I hope you're not coming down with something?'

'No, just a bit of a nervous stomach,' replied Grindal.

'You're not worried about the meeting tomorrow night are you Grandad?'

Josh rolled his eyes upwards in a mock show of innocence.

Grindal knew that Josh had hit the mark with his comment, but there was no way he would ever admit it. The thought of attending the meeting of the Brotherhood of the Second Coming the following night was really making Grindal nervous.

He stared back at Josh with a big false grin on his face.

'No, as a matter of fact, I'm quite looking forward to it. I was also thinking that it might be a good idea if you joined us.'

'That would be really nice if you did Josh. I'm sure you would enjoy it.' Clare seemed quite excited with the proposition of getting both father and son into the same meeting.

'Have you ever attended one of your mother's meetings?' asked Grindal.

Josh looked dumbfounded. He stared at his mother and then back to Grindal.

'Well as a matter of fact I haven't. Mum knows how busy I am with schoolwork and stuff. We discussed it ages ago and Mum agreed that if I didn't want to go to the meetings, I didn't have to.'

'Yes, that is true Dad, we did agree,' said Clare.

'Well I think that's really wise and considerate of your mother to give you the choice Josh. Don't you think that a nice way of thanking her would be to come along to tomorrow night's meeting? We can enjoy the experience together.'

Grindal smiled across the table at Josh refusing to disconnect his eye contact.

Josh started to squirm in his chair. 'But I'm supposed to be meeting Matthew tomorrow night and besides, you said I didn't have to go if I didn't want to.' Josh looked towards his mother for support.

'You're not scared, are you?' asked Grindal.

'Course not. Why should I be scared?'

'Good, then that's settled. You and I will enjoy the

experience together.' Grindal's face lit up in a triumphant grin.

Before Josh could reply, Clare sealed the invitation by going around the table and giving him a big hug. 'You'll really enjoy it,' she said excitedly.

Josh left the house without offering his usual 'see ya later' to Grindal this did not bother Grindal. He was consoled by the fact that at least he would not be suffering alone. However, it did not stop the queasy feeling that he still had in the pit of his stomach. He was really annoyed with his inability to control such a stupid emotional response. After everyone had left, Grindal decided he would go and discuss his problem with his friend Garth.

The morning was cold as Grindal set off brusquely to the newsagent. Within ten minutes the round trip was completed. Grindal knocked on the Bender's front door then opened it and walked into the hallway.

'Anybody home?'

'Come in Falcon,' came the shout from the kitchen.

Grindal walked into the kitchen. The Benders' were sitting at the table still eating breakfast. He was slightly embarrassed by the fact that they were still wearing pajamas.

Grindal looked quickly at his wristwatch, it was only five past nine.

'I'm sorry, I didn't realise it was so early,' he blurted out.

'Never mind that Grindal. Come and sit down and have some coffee.' Tulip gave him her usual big smile.

Grindal sat at the table. Garth helped himself to his newspaper and flipped quickly through the pages. Within five minutes he was finished.

'I really don't know why you waste your money on this right-wing rag,' said Garth shaking his head. 'It's full of advertisements and apologies for the government.'

'Don't be a left-wing snob, Bender,' said Tulip. 'If the poor man brought in a copy of the 'Radical Green,' you'd be telling him he was out of touch with modern day society.

'You're probably right,' said Garth. 'Sorry Falcon, you're entitled to read any kind of paper you like.'

'That's all right Garth. It's probably written for people like me, who have no sense of discrimination. Apart from that, I like the sports page.'

Garth leaned back in his chair and sipped on his coffee. 'Now, tell us what brings you out so early on such a cold morning?'

'As a matter of fact, I do have a small problem,' said Grindal. 'Remember a couple of weeks ago when I told you about this religious group my daughter belongs to.'

'You mean the Brotherhood of the Second Coming,'
said Tulip?

'Yes.... Well tomorrow night there is a meeting at my
daughter's place and I'm the special guest. I can't think why,
but I'm really nervous about it. I don't know whether to sit
there and say nothing, tell them what I think, or just play the
game and join in.'

'What do they talk about at their meetings?' asked
Garth.

'To be honest, I'm not really sure. They sing hymns
and do a lot of praying, I suppose. Maybe they talk about the
Second Coming?'

'So, what's the problem?'

'The problem is, I know what will happen. Brother
James, the head honcho will say something I don't like and
the whole meeting will end up in an argument. Quite frankly
there is nothing I would like better than to tell him where to
stick his second coming. But then Clare will be upset and
then Kate, my granddaughter will be upset and so on. To
make matters worse I conned my Grandson Josh into
attending for the first time. I'm sure he'd love me to make a
balls-up of it. So, I'm not really sure what to do.'

Garth took out his pouch of marihuana and rolled his
first joint for the day. After two long sucks, he closed his
eyes for a few seconds to savor the moment.

'What you need is a plan of action.' Garth took another long suck. 'If you have a plan of action and stick to it, no matter what, you'll be in control.'

'What exactly did you have in mind?' asked Grindal.

'Let's play a bit of "The Bard" while we work it out.' Garth went to the sitting room put on his favorite record and returned to the kitchen. The main rooms of the house all had speakers connected to the record player. The muted sounds of "Universal Soldier" filled the kitchen as Garth and Grindal discussed the plan of action.

Several suggestions were put forward, mostly by Grindal himself. These included, feigning a heart attack in order to get the meeting canceled. Direct confrontation. Even pretending to be possessed by an evil spirit. However, it was quickly decided that such actions would probably have negative outcomes and would not solve any ongoing problems.

Three Bob Dylan albums and several cups of coffee later, Garth concluded that the problem was not with the Brotherhood or Brother James, but with Grindal himself.

'You're totally prejudiced and fucking intolerant Falcon. You should be ashamed of yourself.' Garth accentuated his words slightly due to the effects of the marihuana.

Grindal was somewhat disappointed with the outcome of the planning session but on reflection, decided that Garth's considered opinion was probably correct. In the end, it was decided that the best solution was for Grindal to keep quiet and try not to be provoked by anything that might be said. Grindal agreed and decided that although the planning session had come to nothing, at least the discussion had highlighted the fact that his own negative attitude was probably the greatest contributing factor in the whole situation.

******

When Friday evening came around Grindal was feeling slightly apprehensive but the decision to be totally non-reactive, at least gave him a point on which to focus his anxiety. He had put on his best clothes just show everyone he was taking the meeting seriously. Josh was moping around the house grumbling to himself. Clare was in the kitchen with Kate. They were preparing her distinctive recipe of Irish stew which was evidently a favorite with the members of the group, especially Brother James.

Grindal busied himself placing the chairs in the sitting room. A carver chair was reserved for Brother James, this was placed so that it faced the others. A large crucifix carved out of oak and almost three feet high was placed above the mantlepiece behind Brother James' chair. This was normally kept in Clare's bedroom and was only brought out for the meetings of the Brotherhood. It took both Grindal and Josh to hoist it into position.

'If that falls on his head he won't have to wait long to go to heaven,' said Josh.

'Don't be disrespectful,' said Grindal with a smile. 'Who knows, maybe we might learn something from our Brother James.'

'I doubt it,' replied Josh.

There was a special tape of hymns which was played as the group arrived. Grindal was asked by his daughter to cue this up on the tape recorder. It was not until he had struggled for several minutes that he admitted failure and asked Josh to give him a hand. For Grindal, operation of such modern technology was something he found difficult to fathom. So many different buttons and symbols without instructions.

He had tried to find out from Clare what was to be the format of the meeting but apart from the usual hymns and prayers, Clare was unable to tell him. Evidently there were opening prayers followed by a hymn and then a discussion. The topic to be discussed was always chosen by brother

James. This was usually the finer point of one of the miracles or the main reason for a particular event. In the end Grindal decided that worrying about what might happen was pointless. He stood in the doorway of the small sitting-room and surveyed the scene before him. In the dim light, the imposing presence of the large crucifix gave a somber atmosphere to the room. 'Not much heavenly joy in here,' he said to himself.

Just before seven, there was a knock on the door which announced the arrival of the first members of the group. Grindal followed his instructions and pressed the play button on the tape recorder.

The response took him completely by surprise. The sound of clanging guitars and beating drums jumped out of the speakers with deafening clarity. Grindal pounced on the machine and frantically started to turn knobs and press buttons which might make the noise disappear, but everything he did seemed to be of no avail. Clare rushed into the room wearing a look firstly of shock and then anger. She turned down the volume and changed the tape from howling guitars to the gentle lilt of harps and organs.

'Whoops . . . Sorry about that Clare. I was sure I had the tape you gave me in there. You know me, hopeless with this new electrical stuff.'

'Maybe I should have asked Josh,' said Clare with a frown.

Josh was standing at the door directly behind Clare with a big grin on his face which told Grindal exactly how the tapes had been mixed up. Meanwhile, the knocking on the door was becoming more impatient.

Clare opened the door to the first three members to arrive. They were shivering cold having left their coats in the car. There were two elderly women and a middle- aged man.

'Sorry about that Doris', said Clare. 'We had a little problem with the tape recorder.'

'That's all right, just show me the heater,' replied Doris with a smile.

Doris looked askance at Grindal who was standing next to Clare.

'Doris, this is my father, Grindal.'

Grindal offered his hand and then repeated the gesture as he met Gwen and Frank.

Grindal judged that all three were, probably the same age as himself. The two women were dressed almost identically in black two-piece suits. Frank's distinguishing features were a completely bald head, and a very large nose. Clare called out to Josh who had now disappeared into the kitchen.

'Come and meet our guests Josh.'

Josh walked slowly down the passage and offered what Grindal observed to be a rather wilted handshake to the guests. He then stood in silence as the, 'what a big boy' and 'looks just like his mother,' comments were passed between the new arrivals.

'Why don't you all go into the sitting room and get warmed up? Dad and Josh will look after you while I finish in the kitchen,' said Clare.

Grindal and Josh dutifully led the way into the sitting room and indulged in small talk for the few minutes it took before the next group arrived.

'I'll get that,' offered Doris.

A few minutes later the room was filled with people. Grindal was introduced to each of them in rapid succession. Most were elderly and spoke in lowered voices as they entered the sitting-room. Some even crossed themselves and bowed before the crucifix before they took their seats. There was however one younger woman in the group. She had brought her daughter along with her. Kate and the other young girl seemed to be well acquainted. The pair of them immediately disappeared into the bedroom. Grindal hoped they would stay there. He didn't want his granddaughter to see him make a fool of himself if there were any problems in the meeting.

The group waited patiently for their leader as they discussed the weather and other mundane issues. Grindal sat quietly and watched them. Suddenly there was a loud squeal from the doorway. Grindal looked up to see Bruce, the dog, as he bounded into the room. He was wet and his paws were covered in mud. Bruce ran around the room excitedly jumping up onto the laps of the surprised guests. Grindal leaped to his feet and chased Bruce around the room. Eventually he captured him and dragged him by the collar towards the back door.

Clare busied herself with a damp sponge wiping muddy paw marks from black suits and grey trousers. Her apologies were readily accepted by the now, much more animated members of the congregation.

Grindal looked at Josh as he opened the backdoor. 'I wonder who let the dog inside?' Josh just smiled and shook his head.

It was cool outside as Grindal ushered the dog into its kennel. He was tempted to give Bruce a kind word and a pat on the head but managed to restrain himself he did not want the dog to get the wrong idea. He decided instead to stretch his legs and wandered slowly down the side of the house. As he came close to the front garden, he heard a voice and realised quickly that it was someone talking on the telephone.

Grindal peeked around the corner, and sure enough there was the imposing figure of Brother James talking animatedly into a mobile telephone. He pulled back and stood quietly unobserved as he listened to what appeared to be a fairly intense conversation.

'Look, I've got to have some. Don't fuck me about. If money's a problem, I might be willing to pay a bit more.'

There was a silence as Brother James listened to the voice on the other end.

'That's better, that's what I want to hear. Now be a dear and bring it around to my place tomorrow night.' Brother James finished his call.

Grindal retreated quickly down the side of the house. He went swiftly through the back door and into the sitting room as Clare was greeting Brother James at the front entrance.

A hush descended over the group as he came into the room. Brother James was a large imposing figure with a deep bass ring to his voice. He had a piercing gaze that one sometimes sees in pictures of saints and madmen. He was dressed immaculately in an expensive looking navy-blue suit with a white shirt and red tie. All the members of the gathering lined up in an ordered fashion in front of their chairs. Brother James stood before them. He raised his hands above his head as if reaching out towards the heavens.

'God be with you all,' he said with a commanding voice. He then sat down.

The rest of the group followed.

Brother James smiled. 'I see we have some new members in our group.' He cast his eyes first upon Josh, who had taken a chair as far as possible from the leader of the group. Then he looked directly at Grindal who had seated himself off to one side. His smile faded.

'Welcome to our group Mr. Falcon. May the Lord bless you and give you the strength and humility to be subservient to his will?' Brother James stared at Grindal as if expecting some reaction.

Grindal smiled and held his gaze.

'God bless you too.'

The conversation he had heard a few minutes earlier, made Grindal feel much better. He knew now that he was looking at a very ordinary man. Not the visionary his daughter had described, but something else.

'Let us pray,' commanded brother James.

Grindal watched as the people in the room lowered their heads and closed their eyes. From where he was sitting, he could cast his eyes over the whole group. It always amazed him to watch devout people pray. To him they seemed subservient and afraid. There was no happiness, no fulfilment.

His parents had been strict Catholics. He had attended a catholic school. He remembered the beatings he had endured, for not being able to recite the Catechism. Grindal had decided in his early teens that religion was used as a control mechanism. His mother was terrified of the priest and his father had been deferential. They had been indoctrinated from an early age, filled with fear of being cast into hell for the slightest sin. Grindal's moment of illumination had come one Sunday after mass when the local priest had called him into the vestry and then made some sexual suggestions that had first surprised and then disgusted him. The priest was smelling of liquor and was annoyed when Grindal refused his advances. Ever since that day he had been openly hostile towards anyone and anything to do with religion.

As Grindal surveyed the group before him, he felt sorry for them. What were they looking for? What was his daughter looking for? He watched her praying fervently. She was sitting with the man called Gerry whom Grindal had met previously. Josh, his grandson sat with eyes wide open looking at his wristwatch. He looked up and saw Grindal watching him. As their eyes met, Grindal offered a small grin. Josh reciprocated and then quickly looked away.

Grindal had not been listening to the prayer. He turned his eyes towards Brother James and realised that he had been watching him stare around the room.

'Amen.'

The prayer had come to an end. The two men eyed each other for a few seconds.

Grindal had the distinct feeling that he was involved in some kind of power struggle without knowing why.

Brother James sat erect in the chair and stared around the room.

'We shall now sing,' he announced.

His deep bass voice filled the room as he began to sing. 'Rock of ages cleft for me let me hide myself in thee . . .' The rest of the congregation joined him with great enthusiasm.

As the hymn ended, Brother James raised his hand in a silent command for quiet. He then waited a few seconds before he spoke.

'Our discourse tonight will be on, 'The second coming and the end of the world. There was a stillness as everyone waited for him to continue.

'Matthew 24:27 states that the return of Christ will be like the brightness of lightning illuminating the entire sky from the east to the west.'

'The faithful shall be rewarded when Christ returns. God's kingdom shall be established, and sinners will be cast into the fires of hell.'

There was a long silence as Brother James waited for his words to sink in.

'Will the dead rise?'

The question was raised by one of the elderly women in the group.

'Yes, but only the ones who have been baptized and believe in the Lord,' came the authoritative reply from Brother James.

He stared across at Grindal as he gave the reply.

'I've been baptized,' offered Grindal, returning the stare. He was finding it hard to believe the question and the answer he had just heard.

'Glad to hear it, Brother Grindal.'

Was there a hint of sarcasm in that reply?

Brother James then proceeded to tell the assembled group in intricate detail about life after death, the second coming and the end of the world. Grindal watched and listened. The people in the room were enthralled. They sat spellbound as they heard of angels and golden citadels. Of the earth being destroyed by fire.

All the true believers, especially the group present,

would be taken up in floating palaces while the unbelievers were incinerated back on earth. The earth would then be magically restored in seven days. A new hierarchy would then be installed. God would be in charge and would oversee things from heaven. Jesus would run things back on earth.

Grindal watched the faces of the gathering. Did they truly believe what they were being told? He answered his own question. They must do, otherwise why would they be sitting here? He did not feel any anger or resentment towards them. They were just ordinary people searching for something. To be intolerant of these people would be like being intolerant towards children who believe in Father Christmas. Even the strange man leading them regarded himself as one of the chosen ones. Grindal felt less charitable towards Brother James. There was something about the man he didn't like, although he couldn't quite put his finger on it.

Grindal had to admit, the man was a great storyteller. He had the group convinced that all the information he gave them was passed on directly by one of the angels who visited him in his dreams. As the revelation came to an end, Brother James closed his eyes for a few seconds as if commuting with some unseen presence.

'Are there any questions?' he asked the group.

Grindal couldn't resist, he had to have at least one

little dig.

'Will you be helping Jesus when he comes back to earth?' he asked seriously.

Brother James eyed him suspiciously.

'If the Lord deems me worthy, I will of course do my best to assist him.'

'Yes' I thought you might,' said Grindal under his breath.

'And now let us pray, that the Lord Jesus will accept our worship and forgive our sins, so that we may be saved from the fires of hell.'

Everyone in the room except Grindal and Brother James closed their eyes tightly and prayed fervently, lest they be seen as unworthy and unrepentant.

It crossed Grindal's mind that for all the bible reading he had done in his youth, he could not recall anywhere, where Christ asked people to worship him. He listened as Brother James sowed the seeds of fear and damnation. When the prayer finished everyone sat quietly. Each no doubt reflecting on the sins they had committed both past and present.

What a miserable bunch, not one spark of joy in the whole room.

Brother James took control. He gave them permission

to be happy.

'And now Brothers and Sisters, let us rejoice and break bread with The Lord.'

He smiled and raised his arms. The group before him looked up, saw his smiling face and knew they had been forgiven. The atmosphere in the room changed as if by magic.

This man's dangerous. Grindal watched what he perceived to be the total manipulation of everyone in the room.

Clare stood up. 'I'll get supper,' she said.

'Let me help you,' said Josh. He stood quickly and followed his mother to the kitchen. Grindal was surprised by the offer but then thought it might be a good excuse to leave the room and decided to follow.

The Irish Stew had been warming in the oven. Clare set out the bowls and proceeded to fill each one with a portion of the stew. There was one bowl which was slightly larger than the rest. 'The blue one's for Brother James,' said Clare. 'Irish stew is his favorite.'

Josh placed six bowls of stew onto a tray, including the large one. As he turned his back on his mother to pick up the tray, he slipped his hand into his pocket and pulled out a handful of seeds and herbs. These he quickly sprinkled on top of the stew in the large bowl. Just as he did so, Grindal entered the kitchen and caught him in the act. Josh held his finger up to his mouth. Grindal did not respond and was not quite sure what he had just observed.

'Can I help you with those, Josh?'

'Thanks, Grandad, maybe you can give out some of the bowls of stew? The blue one is for Brother James. Irish Stew is his favorite.'

Grindal smiled.

'Don't worry Josh, I'll make sure he gets the blue one.' He took the tray and handed out the contents to the congregation.

Within ten minutes everyone in the room was tucking into the Irish Stew. Space was limited so most of the group held their bowls in one hand and a spoon in the other. Those who couldn't manage, sat at a small oval table, which was used on special occasions. Brother James was one of these. Grindal watched him as he scoffed down the food with obvious relish. He began to wonder what Josh had put in the stew. At first, he thought it might be something more than extra pepper or salt, but Brother James seemed to be showing no ill effects to whatever it might have been. Josh in turn had been staying close to the congregation which meant that Grindal did not get a chance to ask him. Grindal dismissed the matter from his thoughts and pondered on what might be offered in the second half of the evening.

With teacups and stew bowls cleared away, the group was called to prayer by Brother James. Grindal watched him carefully. Brother James was as serious as ever. Grindal listened to the supplication which was offered to the congregation with great enthusiasm.

'And when Christ returns, the chosen ones will be sought out. The holy spirit will descend on them and they will be filled with joy.' Brother James stopped and looked slowly around the room. Suddenly his face lit up with a wide beaming smile. This was immediately followed by a huge guffaw. Within seconds Brother James was rolling in his seat unable to contain himself. It was as if he had just heard the funniest joke in the world. The small congregation watched with eyes agog at the unfamiliar antics of their leader.

'It must be the Holy Spirit. The Holy Spirit has descended on Brother James,' shouted Doris from the back of the room.

'Hallelujah,' came another cry. Grindal recognised the voice of his Grandson who was now wearing a huge grin. Grindal watched the faces of the group as they transformed from sinners to winners. The laughter was contagious, soon everyone in the room was laughing along with the leader.

Brother James suddenly stopped laughing and pulled a very serious face. When the others saw this, they also stopped their laughter and waited like children to be admonished.

'Blessed be The Lord,' shouted Brother James as he raised his arms above his head. But then he lost his composure and doubled up again in uncontrollable laughter.

'It's a miracle,' shouted Gwen.

'Hallelujah,' shouted Josh, who was now enjoying himself enormously.

Gerry left Clare's side and walked over to Brother James, who was now rolling on the floor, hands clasped around his stomach.

'It must be a miracle; I've never seen him laugh like this before. Normally he hardly ever smiles,' said Gerry to no one in particular.

The smiles and laughter from the rest of the group were now wearing a bit thin. It seemed that Brother James had been blessed with something they could only observe but not participate in. The group now gathered around and watched their leader who was still on the floor and as jolly as ever. At last Brother James calmed down slightly and tried to speak to the now perplexed audience surrounding him.

'I ca... st... I cst. la...' The words sputtered out but did not make sense.

'He's speaking in tongues,' shouted Doris.

'Hallelujah,' came the familiar sound of Josh, who was immediately chastised by his mother, who was now, not amused.

'Somebody pick him up,' said Clare loudly. Grindal walked over to Brother James and bent over him in order to lift him off the floor.

'You bastard Falcon, you spiked my food!'

No one else was close enough to hear the comment. Grindal looked at Brother James' face. The mouth was smiling but the eyes were deadly serious.

'Not me Brother,' he whispered in reply.

'Gerry, give Dad a hand will you. Put him back in the chair,' said Clare.

Gerry did as he was told, and between the two of them they managed to lift Brother James back into his chair. An elderly gentleman called George fetched a glass of water and tried to get Brother James to drink it. After three failed attempts, he decided to throw it into his face.

This unexpected action silenced everyone in the room. It also had the desired effect on Brother James and reduced his raucous laughter to intermittent giggles.

'I'm sorry, everyone,' sniggered Brother James. 'I

don't know what's come over me. I just can't seem to keep a straight face.'

'It's the Spirit. It must be the Holy Spirit,' said Doris. 'You were talking about it just before you were possessed.'

'If it is, then I must pray to the Lord that he doesn't fill me with so much of it in future,' said Brother James, still wearing a beaming smile. 'Perhaps a cup of coffee, Sister Clare if you don't mind. Actually, I feel quite embarrassed. But I suppose I should feel privileged that The Lord should deem me worthy of such an honor.'

Grindal smiled, he now guessed that his grandson had added a lot more than salt to the stew. Brother James convinced everyone that he had been touched by The Holy Spirit. The rest of the group fell in line when their leader pointed out that they too were privileged, by bearing witness to the event. Grindal looked at his daughter, whilst she was nodding in assent Grindal thought he detected a small element of doubt in her demeanor. *Let's hope she never finds out. That would be the end of Josh as far as she's concerned.*

He walked back into the kitchen and motioned Josh to follow.

'Jesus Josh, what the hell did you put in the stew?'

'A few magic beans, I got from one of the boys. They really hit the spot, didn't they?'

'Christ, you could have killed him,' said Grindal

'You're not kidding, I thought he was going to die laughing.'

'If your mother finds out, you'll be dead meat,' said Grindal now more seriously.

'Yeah, I know,' said Josh. 'You won't say anything, will you?'

Grindal shook his head in disbelief. 'Don't worry, I won't dob you in. But promise me you won't do it again?'

Josh just laughed.

When they returned to the sitting room, the group was breaking up. Brother James had decided to close the meeting early. Because he was still feeling too jolly for his own good, it was decided that Gerry would drive him home and he would pick up his car the following day. Grindal decided it might be a good idea if he were out when Brother James returned the following day.

As soon as everyone had left, Grindal informed Clare that he was feeling really tired and would go straight to bed. He had decided it might not be a good idea to get into any deep discussions on the events of the night. He did not want to be put in the position where he had to tell lies to his daughter. Josh was already in bed; he too had disappeared as quickly as possible when everyone had left.

Grindal stood under the hot shower and reflected on the outcome of the evening's activities. After turning the events over in his mind for a few minutes, he came to the conclusion that no harm was done, and everyone had ended up a winner. All in all, he was quite pleased.

The following morning Grindal, Josh and Kate were sitting at the kitchen table. Because It was Saturday, Clare was in no hurry to rush through breakfast. It was customary on Saturdays for everyone to have a large breakfast and a light lunch. Clare was eager to discuss with her father the events of the evening before. She had tried earlier, but Grindal had brushed off the event and tried to change the subject.

'What do you think happened to him?' asked Clare.'

'Who?' said Grindal casually.

'Brother James of course. I've never seen anything like it. Rolling round on the floor laughing like that. What could have caused it?'

'Maybe it was your Irish Stew Mum,' said Kate. 'You said it was his favorite.'

Grindal looked at Josh in alarm.

'I don't think so,' said Josh quickly. 'Grandad gave him the stew, and it was the same as everyone else had. Maybe he's been on some kind of tablets and they affected him.'

'It seems very strange,' said Clare thoughtfully. 'What do you think Dad?'

Grindal reflected for a moment. *Why not take the line of least resistance?*

'Maybe it was the Holy Spirit. He's serious about his faith. Perhaps he was overcome with a surge of emotion.'

'He's coming to pick up his car in an hour. Maybe we can discuss it together,' said Clare.

'I've got an appointment at the hairdressers,' said Grindal quickly. 'Anyway, I'm sure it's nothing serious. In any case, he seemed to be quite pleased with the event last night.'

'I suppose so,' said Clare.

Grindal and Josh exchanged glances. Grindal himself was beginning to feel guilty about lying to his daughter. Anyway, it was done now and there was nothing he could do about it. He had earlier made his grandson repeat his promise not to interfere ever again with the activities of Brother James or the rest of the group, and if possible, he would excuse himself from any further meetings.

'Kate, would you like to come to the shopping centre with Grandad while he has a haircut?'

'Can I Mum?'

'As long as Grandad doesn't fill you up with chocolate,' answered Clare.

Grindal winked at his granddaughter.

'Grandad doesn't do that does he Kate?'

After breakfast Grindal made a swift exit along with his granddaughter. He needed a haircut and luckily for him there was not too many people in the hairdressers, sometimes, you actually did need an appointment on a Saturday morning.

After the haircut, they went to the espresso bar where Grindal ordered a strong cup of coffee. Kate had a cream doughnut and a hot chocolate. Kate was excited about the annual school concert. She was to play the part of a fairy queen and she had lots of lines to learn. Grindal promised faithfully that he would come to see her in the show. He was learning to like being a Grandad and was now realizing what he had missed out on through his stubborn attitude.

When they arrived home, Brother James had already left. Clare told Grindal that he had completely recovered from his experience. He was convinced that he had been visited by the Holy Spirit and filled with joy. This he believed was a reward for the work he had done for The Lord. Grindal smiled and shook his head in acknowledgment.

The following day he visited the Benders'. Garth had a good laugh when Grindal told him about the meeting of

The Brotherhood. Even Grindal had to agree, the plan of non-action had worked out perfectly.

******

CHAPTER 11

O ver the following three weeks, Grindal spent most days
on his own. The Benders' had gone off to Sydney
supposedly to attend a convention on the environmental
effects of global warming. This, Garth had explained to him,
enabled them to have a tax-deductible holiday. Grindal had
worked out very quickly that Garth was very adept at
manipulating the system in all kinds of ways.

Clare had committed her spare time to helping with the
up-coming school concert. There were costumes to make,
and lots of rehearsals to attend. Josh, for a change was busy
studying for the end of term exams. Grindal gave himself
some of the credit for this change in attitude as far as study
was concerned. He had pointed out to Josh that had he spent
more time studying in his youth, instead of drinking and
chasing girls, he might not now be sharing a bedroom with
his grandson.

This was no lie. It was a fact that Grindal had regretted
most of his life that he had not made more of himself. His
own stubborn attitude had prevented him from taking
advantage of the intelligence he had been born with.
Although he had very rarely ever been out of work, he had

always regarded himself as an under achiever. Of late, Grindal had found himself to be more introspective. He spent a lot of time thinking about how his life had changed since Jessie had died. Those few short months had taught him many things. On reflection, he concluded that he was now less self-centered and more tolerant than he had been previously. In the first few weeks there had been a fire in him that had burned angrily. The flames were still there, but not nearly as bright as they had been.

He still thought about Jessie and their life together, but the thoughts that were once so immanent were now less demanding. Where once they were coupled with resentment and loss they were now clothed in sentiment and melancholy. He was more able to control this new attitude. Any gloom or despair he felt, soon disappeared with a visit to the park with his granddaughter or better still, a long cup of coffee with the Benders'. He was reminded of the statement made by Roy, the man who had rescued him the night his house burned down. 'Broken hearts are like broken bones; with time they repair themselves. The secret is, to forget the pain of the actual break.'

It was when he was thinking about this that Grindal decided he should revisit Roy and apologise for running off without saying a word. It was something he had thought about before. It played on his mind. Grindal knew he had done the wrong thing by him. The fact that Roy was a poofter was no excuse. Having made the decision Grindal decided he should act on it immediately. There was something else he also determined he would do.

That evening he found Roy's telephone number and after some hesitation made the call. He crossed his fingers hoping that Roy's friend Damien didn't pick up the phone.

'Hello.'

'Hello, Roy?'

'Yes'

'Grindal here. Grindal Falcon.'

There was a short silence on the other end of the telephone before Roy answered.

'I didn't think I'd hear from you again.'

'Yes, I know,' said Grindal. 'I've been thinking about how I left your place without saying a word. I feel bad about it and I'd like to apologise. Do you mind if I come around and see you? I'd really like to talk to you if I can? I thought tomorrow, if that's all right with you?'

There was another short silence.

'Ok, make it after lunch, about two.'

'Fine, I'll see you then.'

Grindal put down the receiver slowly. He was nervous

about the appointment he had just made but determined to keep it.

The following day he caught the bus to the shopping centre. It was not long before he found what he was looking for.

Cromwell Real Estate Agents had a large shop front office adjacent to the main shopping area. When Grindal walked in he was greeted with a smile by the man behind the counter.

'Good morning sir. Can I help you?'

'Yes, I hope so,' said Grindal. 'I've got a block of land I'd like to sell.'

'In that case, I'm sure we can be off assistance.' The salesman held out his hand to Grindal. 'David Conan.'

Grindal reciprocated. 'Grindal Falcon.'

David Conan rubbed his hands together as he guided Grindal to a small desk behind the counter area.

'Now where exactly is it, Mr. Falcon?'

'Forty-seven, Harris Street Newport West,' answered Grindal.

'Oh, I know the one. Is that the one where the house burned down?'

'Yes,' replied Grindal without explanation.

'Was that yours, the house I mean?' asked the surprised

Salesman.

'Yes, it was. But never mind that. It's for sale now and I need someone to organize it for me. Do you think you can handle that?'

Grindal was becoming a little impatient. He didn't want a conversation with the man. He just wanted to get on with it. David Conan was a professional and quickly picked up the slight edge in his customer's voice. This was no time to bring up unfortunate memories.

'Actually, land in that area is becoming quite valuable, with the new Westgate Bridge going up.'

'How valuable?'

'About twenty thousand for a block that size.'

Grindal was dumbfounded. twenty thousand dollars. He had no idea it was worth that much. When he and Jessie had bought it, they had paid a few hundred pounds.

The man opposite took the few seconds of silence for a negative response.

'We might get twenty- five if we auction it,' he said hopefully.

'I suppose that's not too bad,' said Grindal, now more in control. 'What do you suggest?'

Within ten minutes, he had signed up an exclusive agent's agreement for the next three months. The land would be put on the market for twenty-two thousand two hundred and fifty dollars, with the good expectation that it would fetch at least twenty. Grindal was more than pleased with the figure. Even with agents' fees taken out, he would still be left with a tidy sum.

The next place he visited was the bottle shop where he picked up a bottle of scotch which he hoped would lend some strength to his apology.

Grindal was more than a little nervous when he knocked on the front door of Roy's house. He felt better when Roy greeted him with a smile.

'Come in.'

Grindal nodded his head and walked into the house and down to the kitchen. He handed Roy the bottle.

'Something to put in the grog cupboard,' he said awkwardly.

'Thanks,' said Roy taking the bottle. 'Would you like a beer or a coffee?' he added.

'Coffee would be fine,' said Grindal.

Roy had his back to Grindal as he prepared the two cups of coffee. 'So how have you been?' he said, trying to lessen the nervous tension he could feel coming from Grindal.

'Look, I won't mess about, the reason I'm here is to

apologise for leaving the way I did,' Grindal blurted out. 'I feel really bad about it, especially after what you did for me and all. But I didn't realise you were a.....'

'A poofter,' said Roy, as he sat down opposite Grindal.

'Well it was a bit of a surprise. And when you and your friend started. You know. It sort of caught me off balance. Then one thing led to another and off I went.'

Grindal looked down at the table unable to look the other man in the eye.

'And what do you think now? Do you still think I'm some sort of pervert?'

'No,' replied Grindal truthfully. 'It's just that at my age you tend to get set in your ways. To be honest It's not something I've really thought about, never mind discussed with anyone. When I was growing up my old man used to say that all queers should be put down. On top of that I had a minor problem with the local priest. Since then I've had this sort of phobia against . . . you know.'

'What did he try to touch you on the arse?' said Roy, with a smile?

'Who?'

'The local priest. Did he try to pat you on the bottom?'

'Something like that,' Grindal blushed.

With that the ice was broken. Within a few minutes the

two men were talking like old friends. Grindal told Roy about his experiences after he had left. They both had a good laugh about Mrs. Fromp and the characters at the boarding house. Roy was especially interested that Grindal had become friends with people like the Benders', who, from Grindal's description, he would certainly enjoy meeting.

'Looks like you two have made up,' said Damien.

The bottle of Scotch Grindal had brought with him was half empty when Roy's friend Damien arrived. He did not acknowledge Grindal.

'Hello,' said Roy. 'Want to join us for a drink.

Damien poured himself a large drink from the bottle of whisky. 'And how is Mr. Falcon doing these days?' he added.

The cool reception from Damien was not lost on Grindal.

'As a matter of fact, I came around to apologise to Roy for the way I ran off without saying anything. If you'll accept it, I'd like to extend that apology to you too.'

Although it was not his intention to do this, Grindal thought it might be appreciated by both men.

Damien looked Grindal in the eye for a few seconds before he answered.

'If Roy's happy, then so am I.'

'Thanks,' said Grindal, and offered Damien his hand.

One hour later, the bottle of whisky was empty, and all three men were chatting to each other the way most people do when they've had too much to drink. Grindal was pleased he had faced his homophobic demon even if it was with the help of several scotches. He looked at the clock on the kitchen wall. It was six thirty.

'Shit, look at the time,' he exclaimed! 'Can I make a phone call? Clare will be worried about me.'

'Sure,' said Roy. 'Anyway, why don't you stay for dinner? We've got another guest coming. I'm sure you'll find her really charming.'

'Yes,' laughed Damien, it could be a sort of blind date. As a matter of fact, it's a sort of, special occasion, tomorrow is her birthday.'

Grindal didn't take much convincing, even though he did wonder why a female would want to celebrate her birthday with a pair of poofters. He was on a high from the alcohol he had consumed and was enjoying himself. The thought of kicking on seemed like a good idea. He made his telephone call to Clare and then helped himself to large chunks of cheese while Roy and Damien prepared dinner.

About an hour later the front doorbell rang.

'That must be Jemima,' said Roy.

'I'll get it,' said Damien.

Grindal stood up and brushed the crumbs from the front of his shirt. He waited in anticipation as Damien opened the door.

'Hello darling, come in. You must be frozen, poor dear.'

Grindal watched from the kitchen as Damien greeted Jemima at the front door.

'Come on into the kitchen Jem, there's someone I'd like you to meet.'

'Oh, I do hope he's handsome,' replied Jemima.

The voice sounded deep and sensuous. There was something about it that Grindal found vaguely familiar.

Damien and Jemima walked into the kitchen, hand in hand.

'Grindal, I'd like to introduce you to our friend Jemima.'

The two guests faced each other. Jemima was wearing what appeared to be a long blond wig. Heavy pancake makeup with lots of mascara and rouge covered the round face. Bright red lipstick accentuated the already large mouth. Jemima wore an expensive looking two-piece suit with matching high heeled shoes and handbag. She was very tall and solidly built. Jemima's eyes had that piercing look that one associates with saints or madmen. There was a stony silence as the two guests faced each other. Jemima's mouth opened, but no sound came out. Grindal continued to stare in disbelief. The seconds ticked by as everyone in the room stared first at Grindal and then at Jemima.

It was Grindal who eventually broke the silence, he smiled.

'Good evening Brother James or should I say Jemima . . . Nice to see you up and about so soon after your recent encounter with the Holy Spirit.'

'Aaaahh...' Jemima let out a high-pitched scream before she turned and fled. In the mad scramble to leave the house, she dropped her hand- bag on the floor.

Grindal watched through the open front door as Brother James made his escape. The sprint across the front garden was too much for the high heeled shoes. Brother James let out a loud groan as he fell flat on his face in the wet grass. This did not slow him down for long, in an instant he was back on his feet now carrying both shoes as he limped to his car.

Grindal watched in amazement as Brother James frantically clawed at the locked door of his car. He then turned and saw Grindal watching him from the entrance of the house. With another audible groan Brother James then scurried up the street unable to run fast because of the tight skirt he was wearing. Grindal watched as the shadowy outline carrying a high heeled shoe in each hand disappeared into the darkness.

The smile on Grindal's face soon turned into a deep belly laugh. The feeling of mirth mixed with satisfaction lasted for a full half minute before he turned to face the two bewildered occupants of the house.

When Grindal explained the reason for his laughter and what had just taken place, both Roy and Damien were amazed. As far as they knew, Jemima, or Jim Warrigal, as they knew him when he wore trousers, was an accountant for a local plumbing company. For the next half hour, Grindal sat and listened in astonishment as Damien and Roy described some of the antics that Jim and Jemima used to get up to.

It seemed that Jim had been a transvestite for many years, however, in the past he had always traveled interstate to practice his inclination for cross dressing. Roy explained that it was only on very rare occasions that he indulged himself in his home- town, and then, never in public. Tonight, was one of those special occasions, a sort of birthday treat.

Both Roy and Damien knew that he was involved with

a religious group, but not as a leader of any sort. In any case, they could never work out, how he justified his religious beliefs with his inclination for wild ecstasy parties. Religion was not their scene, so it was not something they had discussed.

In the end, they all had a good laugh. Grindal insisted that he should be given the opportunity to return the handbag. After some hesitation, the others agreed, providing he returned it the following day. Grindal wanted to hang on to it and present it to Brother James at the next meeting of The Brotherhood. Both Roy and Damien thought that this was too cruel and made Grindal promise to keep his word.

The taxi driver that took Grindal home kept staring at him. He couldn't work out why this elderly man in the seat next to him was carrying a handbag and was wearing a permanent grin on his face.

The following day Grindal waited for everyone to leave the house before he removed Brother James' handbag from the bedside draw where he had hidden it. He emptied the contents onto the kitchen table. He had a devilish curiosity of what the bag might contain.

Sure enough, there was a rare mixture of items. A whole battery of makeup along with a large packet of condoms, a set of keys, a wallet containing credit cards, a driver's license, some funny looking purple pills, a large crucifix, and one hundred dollars in cash. The other interesting item was an address book which contained a long list of names and telephone numbers.

Grindal sipped slowly on a cup of coffee as he stared at the driver's license in his hand and wondered what to do about James Francis Warrigal alias Brother James alias Jemima. Should he tell Clare? Should he tell the rest of the group? He had to be very careful. He did not want to hurt anyone with his new information, but on the other hand he thought he now had a duty to stop the religious pretense that was happening. He decided to discuss the matter with his friend Garth. The Benders'' had returned from their trip to Sydney the previous day. He did not trust the feelings of excitement and power that had come over him since his new discovery.

The following day, over a cup of coffee, Grindal related the story of the night before to Garth and Tulip. Even Garth, who was rarely surprised by anything, was somewhat impressed as Grindal ended his story.

'Falcon, that's astonishing. Who would have thought? From the way you described him, I would have pegged him as some kind of control freak. Definitely not a transvestite.'

'Definitely a complex personality,' offered Tulip dryly.

'Yes, that's what I thought', said Grindal, not quite knowing what that meant.

'Clearly a breakthrough in your relationship with him Falcon. In fact, I would go so far as to say he would now be absolutely shitting himself.' Garth stared into his coffee. 'Knowledge is power, as they say. The power is now yours. Thing is, what do you intend to do with it.' Garth took the address book and thumbed through the pages.

'Some fairly illustrious names in here,' said Garth.

'What do you mean,' said Grindal?'

'You probably wouldn't know them, but some are quite well known in their own circles. I wonder if this is a business book or a pleasure book?... Although I can't think for the life of me why an accountant from Galactic Plumbing would associate with some of the people in here.'

'What do you think I should do?'

'Depends what you want to achieve. Do you want to just piss him off? Do you want him to lose his job? Out him with the rest the brotherhood? Anything is possible.'

'I've thought about it,' said Grindal. All I really want is to stop the creep deceiving my daughter, and all those other people for that matter. What an arshole, probably some kind of drug freak.'

'Hmmm,' Garth coughed. He was rolling a joint when

Grindal made the comment.

Grindal smiled. 'You know what I mean. Anyway, I don't want any 'nutter' hanging about my family. Who knows what else he might be into?'

'Well, the way I see it Falcon, all you have to do is phone him up and tell him what you want,' said Garth casually.

'What if he decides to deny everything and just tough it out?' replied Grindal.

'I don't think he's that stupid. That rag you read every morning would kill for a story like that. I can see the headline now. 'Local religious leader exposed as drug- addicted transvestite.'

'Why don't you phone him now?' said Tulip.

'Now?'

'Why not,' said Garth? Get it out of the way. Apart from that, you promised the other two blokes you'd give him back the handbag today anyway.'

'I suppose you're right,' agreed Grindal.

Tulip passed him the telephone. Grindal rummaged through the handbag until he found what he was looking for. A business card.

'James Francis Warrigal, Accounts Manager,' said Grindal out loud.

He dialed the number on the card, a female voice responded.

'Galactic Plumbing, Sophie speaking. How can I help you?'

'I'd like to speak to Mr. Warrigal please?' said Grindal.

'I'm sorry but Mr. Warrigal is in an important meeting right now. Would you care to leave a message and I'll get him to phone you back?'

'I think if you tell him Mr. Falcon would like to speak to him, he'll decide that his meeting is not as important as you might think.'

There was some hesitation on the other end. 'I'll try, but he really hates to be interrupted. I doubt very much if he'll talk to you.'

'Go on, just give it a go. If he doesn't want to speak to me, tell him I'll come around to see him. At his convenience of course,' said Grindal sarcastically.

He waited for about half a minute before he heard the familiar voice of Brother James.

'What do you want?'

He was obviously angry.

'Now, now, James, or should I call you Jemima. I hope I didn't disturb your important meeting. Perhaps if you explained to your colleagues that you lost your handbag last night, and that some kind man wanted to return it.'

'Fuck you Falcon. I knew you were trouble the first time I laid eyes on you. No doubt you're the bastard that spiked my drink the other night.'

'Such language, and from a man of the cloth too. I hope none of the Brotherhood hear you talking like that. They might think you're a fraud.'

'Cut the crap Falcon. What do you want?'

The tone of his voice was somewhat condescending, not at all desperate or fearful of any consequences. Grindal picked this up and immediately lost his temper.

'I'll tell you what I want shithead. I want you to disappear out of my life. I want you to disappear out of the lives of my daughter and my granddaughter. I don't care how you do it, just fucking evaporate.'

'Now who's getting upset,' said the voice on the other end of the telephone. Anyway, as far as I'm concerned you can get fucked. You've got nothing on me. All you have is my wallet and my driver's license which I shall report as lost. Anything else is just your word against mine. I'm sure no one in the Brotherhood is interested in any accounts you might get from two poofters. I think they might be more interested what you were doing with them.'

Grindal was momentarily confused by the confidence of Brother James. Whilst he never expected him to roll over and confess all, he was not ready for a complete denial. He stared across at Garth who was looking through the address book and smiling. It gave him a flash of inspiration. He reached across and grabbed the book from his hands. Grindal opened the book randomly. 'What about George Frazer and Malcom Cuthbert and Rev Armitage. Is that 'The' Reverend Armitage' by the way?'

There was complete silence on the other end of the telephone.

'Would you like me to read a few more out? Or maybe it would be easier if I gave the book to someone in the press. I'm sure they would be interested, especially when I tell them how I came to have the book in my possession.'

The silence from the other end of the telephone was suddenly broken by a string of invective.

'You dirty rotten bastard, you fucking cunt, you fucking arshole.'

Grindal interrupted. 'I see you remembered your address book James. For a minute there, I was beginning to think you didn't care.'

'Alright, Alright, you've made your point. What do you want? I must have that book back.'

Grindal took a deep breath, relieved that he now had the situation under control.

'Can you type James?'

'What the fuck are you talking about,' came the angry reply.

'Well I hope you can, because if you want your book and your other stuff back, I need a letter from you. A sort of written confessional if you know what I mean. And just to make sure you don't accidently bump into anyone; I think it would be a good idea if you went to live somewhere else. The further away the better.'

'That's ridiculous, no way,' said James.

'If you insist, then we'll do it the hard way. Either way I win and to be honest, I think I would prefer it the hard way.'

Grindal was very sure of himself now, he knew exactly what he wanted.

There was another short silence. 'What precisely do you want?' asked Brother James.

'I want a letter addressed to the members of the Brotherhood. In it, I want you to say that you are a fraud, a dope addict and a liar who has been deceiving them ever since the group began. You have a good way with words, I'm sure you can put something together that's suitable.'

'But . . .' came the muffled response from the Brother James.

Grindal interrupted. 'And when you've done that, call a cab to deliver the letter to the red brick house directly opposite my daughters' place, number 47. If the contents of the letter are suitable, then I'll give the cab driver your bag with your stuff in it. If not, then the deals off. And by the way don't fuck me about, you only get one chance.'

Grindal reflected for a moment about his daughter and the rest of the group, they would be devastated. He made another quick decision.

'And just to show you how big hearted I am, you can write your own resignation to the Brotherhood. Say whatever you like. As long as you don't show up, I won't tell them the truth. I'll look forward to the next meeting when they read it out.'

'How do I know you won't copy the book?' asked Brother James.

'You'll just have to take my word for it Brother.'

After a short silence Brother James replied. 'Give me an hour.' There was a loud clunk as he hung up the telephone.

'How did it go?' asked Tulip.

'Good, I think,' replied Grindal.

He filled them in on the details they had not already picked up by listening to his side of the conversation.

Grindal then picked up the address book. 'I just have to do a little job before the cab arrives.'

'What's that?' asked Garth.

'Copy this book of course,' Grindal replied with a smile.

'Don't worry said Garth, I'll do it a lot quicker than you.'

Without being asked. He took the address book and disappeared into his study.

About an hour later the taxicab arrived with the letter Grindal had demanded. Grindal opened the envelope and read the contents. He then passed it to Garth.

'What do you think?'

'Seems to fit the bill.'

Grindal gave the cab driver a brown paper bag which contained the handbag and all its contents. Garth had given Grindal a copy of the address book, which he folded and placed in his back pocket.

'Maybe we're letting him off too easily?' said Grindal.

'Don't push your luck Falcon, replied Garth, 'we don't want him coming after you with an axe, do we?'

******

Several days later, Grindal, Josh, and Kate were sitting at the kitchen table waiting for Clare to dish up the roast chicken they were having for dinner. Clare had barely said a word to the rest of the family for the past two hours. She had received a phone call earlier which had obviously upset her.

'Is anything wrong,' asked Grindal?'

Clare looked at him blankly.

'You seem to be upset about something. Is anything wrong?' Grindal repeated the question.

Clare sat down at the table ignoring the plates of food which were still on the kitchen bench.

'It's Brother James, he's leaving.'

Clare clasped her hands tightly, head bowed, staring unblinking at the sugar bowl in the centre of the table.

'What do you mean, leaving, leaving what?' asked Grindal.

'He's disbanding the group, he's leaving, he's going away. Don't you understand?' Clare replied angrily.

'All right, don't get upset, just calm down and tell us what's happening,' said Grindal.

she stood up and pointed her finger accusingly at Grindal.

'You never liked him anyway. I suppose now you'll be happy. No more meetings, no more Brother James.'

She turned her back on Grindal before he could reply and picked up the dinner plates which were still sitting on the kitchen bench. The first two she put down heavily in front of Josh and Kate. She then picked up the remaining two dinners. In one movement Clare placed her own and at the same time reached across and dropped Grindal's in front of him.

The momentum of the action caused the plate to slide across the table and into Grindal's lap. Instinctively, he pushed back his chair and stood up as the hot gravy burned through his trousers. The plate fell and smashed into several pieces as it hit the tiled floor, leaving a colourful montage of green and brown sludge.

Clare froze, staring in disbelief. The anger that had caused the accident was now transformed into remorse. She burst into tears burying her face in her hands. Although taken by surprise, Grindal was quick to recover. He walked swiftly to his daughter's side and wrapped his arms around her. She returned his embrace and buried her face into his shoulder as the tears flowed down her cheeks.

'I'm sorry,' she cried. 'I really didn't mean that to happen.'

'I know,' said Grindal. 'It was just an accident. Don't worry about it.' He kissed her on the forehead. 'I wasn't very hungry anyway,' he smiled.

Josh in the meantime had begun to clean up the mess on the floor. He looked up at Grindal and then turned away.

'You can have half of mine. Mum always gives me too much anyway.'

'Thanks Josh. I might just get changed first.'

'Come on Clare don't get upset. I'm sure everything will work out.'

Clare forced a smile and stepped away from her father. 'I'm sure your right,' she said, but without any real conviction.

When Grindal returned to the kitchen there was a serving of roast chicken ready for him to eat. Clare Josh and Kate waited for him to sit down.

'God bless this family and the food we are about to eat.' Clare said the short prayer as was her habit before they ate their evening meal together. Her eyes were red and still covered with a watery glaze. Grindal discerned an absence of the usual zeal in the offering.

No one spoke as they slowly ate their food. When they had finished the main course, Kate helped her mother to clear the plates from the table.

'Is Brother James going away Mummy?'

Clare sat down at the table. 'Yes Kate, it seems that Brother James has had a calling from the Lord to go to South

America and work for the less fortunate. He's leaving the day after tomorrow. He called Gerry and asked him to let everyone know what was happening.' Clare shook her head. 'I just can't believe it.'

'Will you see him before he goes?' asked Josh.

'No,' replied Clare softly. 'He told Gerry that it would be better if he went quickly without any emotional goodbyes. Evidently, he left a letter to read to the group at our next meeting.... Who knows, maybe it will be our last.'

'What do you think you will do?' asked Grindal.

'I don't know,' said Clare shaking her head. 'Let's hope that God tells us what to do.'

'I'm sure he will,' said Grindal hopefully.'

There was not much conversation in the household the rest of the evening. Clare acted as if she were in mourning. The rest of the family respected her right to feel sorry for herself. Both Grindal and Josh knew that the Brotherhood filled a big space in her life. On reflection Grindal was still convinced he had handled the situation correctly. He only hoped that Clare and the rest of the group would be able to work things out without the help of Brother James. He didn't believe for one minute that Brother James was going anywhere near South America. South Australia maybe, but, definitely not South America.

He decided it might not be a good idea for him to attend the next meeting of the Brotherhood. He had done enough. It was up to them to work out their own fate.

The following day he decided to visit the Benders'. He had not seen them since the day they discussed how he would handle the return of the handbag. As far as Grindal was concerned the situation was all but resolved and they would probably be interested in the latest developments.

After his usual trip to the local newsagent Grindal knocked on the front door of the Benders' house and was surprised to find no one home. Having nothing else to do he decided to return home, read his newspaper and have a quiet day.

It was late in the afternoon when the telephone rang. Clare and Kate were usually home by this time and Grindal guessed that it was probably his daughter letting him know they were late. Josh had gone straight to his mate's house after school and was not expected home much before eight o'clock that evening.

'Hello. Is that Mr. Falcon?'

'Yes.'

'Mr. Falcon, my name is Joan Edwards, I work with your daughter Clare. 'I'm afraid there's been an accident.'

'What do you mean, an accident?' interrupted Grindal.

There was a moment's hesitation before the woman continued.

'I was giving Clare and Kate a lift to the bus stop and we were hit by a car coming out of a side street. I'm sure she'll be all right.'

The woman on the other end of the telephone blurted out the information in a voice that was tinged with hysteria.

'What do you mean? Where's Clare? where's Kate?' Grindal's heart was now racing as his anxiety increased.

'Kate's with me, she's fine. We're at the Western General. Clare was taken to casualty. We're waiting for the doctor. I'm sure she'll be all right.'

The tone in the woman's voice did not give Grindal any confidence in the wellbeing of his daughter.

'Let me speak to Kate,' said Grindal anxiously.

'Hello,' said the timid voice after a few seconds wait.

'Kate, this is Grandad. Are you all right?'

'Yes, but Mum was all covered in blood. Is she going to die?' Kate let out a wail and started to cry.

'No, no. Mum's going to be fine. Don't cry. Try not to worry. Grandad will be there as soon as I can. Just stay with Mrs. Edwards. Tell her I'm coming straight away.'

He slammed down the receiver and then spent what seemed like forever searching for the telephone number to call a taxi. The yellow pages were nowhere to be found and, in his anxiety, he could not find 'taxi' under the white page listings.

The following fifteen minutes he spent waiting at the front of the house anxiously repeating 'come on, come on,' until finally the cab arrived.

When he rushed into the casualty department of the Western General Hospital, it was crowded. There were two nurses behind the enquiry desk trying to deal with several people. When Grindal tried to jump the queue, he was told brusquely to wait his turn. He nervously conceded, but after waiting in line for only a short time Grindal became frustrated and annoyed. He left the desk and began to roam around the large waiting area looking anxiously for his granddaughter.

'Over here grandad.'

When he heard the voice Grindal turned sharply and spotted Kate as she ran towards him. He bent down and wrapped his arms around her.

'Kate, Kate. Are you all right?'

'You must be Mr. Falcon?'

Grindal looked up from his kneeling position. A somewhat disheveled middle- aged woman held out her hand.

'You must be Mrs. Edwards?' said Grindal.

'Yes...Joan.'

The three of them stood in the middle of the large waiting area. They were surrounded by coughing, sneezing and anxious people who were oblivious of anyone's needs except their own.

'There's some seats over here,' offered Mrs. Edwards.

She led them to the far corner of the room which was slightly less crowded.

Although still apprehensive, Grindal was now more in control of his emotions. The fact that his granddaughter was unharmed, at least physically, had accorded him enormous relief.

'Tell me what happened?' He remained standing. Mrs. Edwards and Kate were now seated.

'It's like I told you on the phone. We were only going to the bus stop and this car came out of nowhere. Slammed right into the side where Clare was sitting.'

'Was she hurt badly?' asked Grindal.

Mrs. Edwards looked at Kate.

'It's hard to say. She was in a lot of pain when they put her in the ambulance. We came here in a second ambulance. After they checked us out, the sister told us to wait and she would let us know what was going on as soon as possible.'

'I'll see if I can find out anything,' said Grindal. He stroked his granddaughter on the head and tried to smile reassuringly.

When he returned fifteen minutes later, he carried with him two bottles of soft drink and a packet of potato chips which he handed over without comment.

'Sister says she's in a pretty bad way. But she's going to be all right', he added hastily. 'Evidently, she's just come out of the operating theatre and gone into intensive care. She said a Doctor Fielding will be out shortly to let us know exactly what her condition is.'

He sat down next to his granddaughter and put his arm around her shoulder.

'Looks like Mum might have to stay here for a few days. But we'll manage,' he added.

Kate did not respond. She stared blankly across the room.

Some twenty minutes later Doctor Fielding introduced himself. He took Grindal to one side whilst he explained Clare's condition. She had a fractured pelvis, a broken nose, cracked ribs and possible head injuries. The full extent of her injuries were not yet clear. She was still unconscious and in the intensive care unit. He advised Grindal to go home and return the next day. Grindal thanked him and shook his hand.

'Is Mum going to be all right? Kate looked at Grindal anxiously.

'Yes, the doctor said she'll be fine. She's asleep now, so rather than disturb her it might be better if we go home and come back in the morning.'

He took Kate by the hand as they walked through casualty and into the main entrance.

'Where's your car?' asked Grindal, as an afterthought.

'It went straight to the crash repairer,' replied Mrs. Edwards.

'How will you get home?' asked Grindal.

'That's all right, I'll catch a cab, there's usually some parked outside.

They looked outside and sure enough there were two Taxis parked close to the entrance. Taking Kate by the hand Grindal walked quickly towards the first car. He tried his best to appear calm and in full control of the situation. Mentally he was in overdrive. A torrent of questions filled his mind, most of them began with, 'What if'?

'I'll give you a ring when I know how Clare is,' said Grindal as he guided Kate into the back seat of the Taxi. It was only when they had driven away, he realised he had not asked for a telephone number.

It was eight thirty in the evening when they arrived

home. The house was in darkness which meant that Josh was still out. Grindal spent the next hour fussing over his granddaughter trying to reassure her that everything was going to be all right. She did not want to eat and settled for a hot drink of Milo and a few biscuits. Kate was very quiet; she had hardly spoken since they had left the hospital.

'Now don't you worry about Mum, I'm sure she'll be fine. Tomorrow, you and I, and Josh, will all go to the hospital and see her. And we won't worry about school either, until everything is sorted out. Ok?'

Kate smiled weakly. 'Are you sure Mum will be alright Grandad?'

'Yes, I'm sure.'

In fact, Grindal was not sure at all, there was a lingering doubt in the back of his mind. What if she's not? What if she's crippled? What if she has brain damage? What if she dies? The what ifs' would not stop coming no matter how hard he tried to control his thinking.

Eventually Kate went to bed. Grindal read her a story. He tried to sound enthusiastic as he read the words on the page, but his heart was not in it.

When he eventually sat down in the lounge room, it was past ten thirty. It was only the that he realised that Josh was still not home. 'Where the hell are you Josh?' he whispered out loud. He turned on the television but could not concentrate on any of the programs. As the minutes ticked away, he had the awful thought that Clare might not be his only problem. 'What if......?' The words were spoken but trailed off as the sound of telephone the interrupted the monotone chatter coming from the television.

'Hello,' said Grindal hesitantly.

'I'd like to speak to Clare Marshall,' said the voice on the other end?

'I'm afraid she's not here. She had an accident earlier today. She's in hospital. Can I help you?'

There was no immediate reply except for an audible sigh. Grindal waited.

'Are you any relation to Josh Marshall?'

'Yes, he's my grandson. Is anything wrong?'

'And your name sir, is?'

'Grindal. Grindal Falcon. As I said, he's my Grandson. Is there a problem? Who are you?'

His heart started to beat faster. Could it be possible? Surely not another accident? He dare not ask the question.

'I'm Sargent Godwin from Footscray Police Station. Your grandson was charged earlier this evening with possession of an illegal substance.'

'Oh, thank Christ for that,' Grindal replied.

He was expecting much worse. A drug charge seemed quite trivial. He breathed a sigh of relief.

'Did you hear me correctly sir? Your grandson has been charged with possession of marihuana.'

'Yes, yes, it's just that I thought there might have been another accident. I hear what you say. What shall I.... I mean what do you want me to do?'

Grindal was confused. As much as he tried, he could not think clearly. It was as if his mind had turned to mush.

'Well, if you don't care what happens to him, we'll transfer him to the youth detention centre, and he can stay there until his trial comes up.'

'Yes, I do care,' interrupted Grindal.

'Then you'd better come and pick him up,' came the caustic reply.

'I'll be there as soon as I can.'

The Sargent hung up the phone before Grindal could say any more. He sat in the chair by the telephone and shook his head in total disbelief. He was no longer perplexed. He was angry.

'Fuckin hell. You fucking stupid idiot Josh. I don't believe it. I just don't believe it. Picked up for carrying drugs. Fuck me. How fucking stupid can you get?'

The torrent of invective helped to relieve his tension.

His head was beginning to clear. He knew he had to keep control of himself if he wanted to manage the situation he was in. He made himself think slowly and precisely. The first thing he had to do was to get down to the police station. *That Sargent Godwin sounded totally pissed off. Definitely, not much help or sympathy coming from that direction.*

Walking quickly down the hallway, he glanced into Kate's room. She was sound asleep. There were two choices. He could wake her up and take her down to the police station or if not, he must get someone to stay with her while he went on his own. He did not want to disturb her. She had been through enough for one day. To wake her and tell her that her brother was being held by the police did not seem like a very good option. But who could he ask to stay with her at that time of the night? His first thought was the Benders', but Kate didn't know the Benders'. If she woke up and found strangers in the house, who knows what might happen. Clare had plenty of friends in the Brotherhood but Grindal did not know them or where they lived.

Finally, he went back to the telephone and thumbed quickly through the Teledex. He took a deep breath and dialed the number.

The telephone was answered almost immediately.

'Hello.'

'Hello Moira. This is Grindal.'

There was a short silence.

'What do you want?'

'I'm sorry to disturb you but I've got a bit of an emergency and I need your help.'

Grindal held his breath. He had not spoken to Moira since the day of the incident at the bowling club. Apart from that, Clare had verbally abused her the morning after. It seemed to take forever before she replied.

'What do you want?' she repeated.

'It's Clare, she was involved in a car accident earlier on today. She's still in hospital. My problem is, that the police have just rung and told me Josh is in some kind of trouble. I have to go and pick him up. I need someone to stay with Kate while I'm away.'

There was a short pause. In the background Grindal could hear Moira talking to someone.

'I will understand if you don't want to help,' he blurted out.

Straight away he wished he hadn't said it. It sounded almost like an apology.

'I'll be there in a minute,' said Moira.

'Thank you.' He breathed a sigh of relief.

'Oh, and by the way, Basil is with me.'

257

Grindal put the phone down.

Fucking Basil. Jesus Christ, that's all I need. He shook his head. Two minutes later there was a knock on the front door.

'Thank you again for coming,' said Grindal.

He looked at Moira and tried to avoid any eye contact with Basil. Despite the situation, Grindal could not help but feel totally embarrassed. *Basil must be really loving this, really gloating,* He could still not make himself look at the man. *Josh, you bastard, wait till I catch up with you.* When they reached the living room Grindal nervously moved cushions off chairs and picked up the newspaper off the floor where he had left it earlier in the day. The three of them stood in silence for a moment, not quite knowing how to start the conversation.

'How is Clare? Is she badly hurt?' asked Moira.

'They're not really sure yet. She has a few broken bones, but there may be some head injuries.'

'Oh dear, I do hope she'll be all right,' said Moira with genuine concern.

'And what about your grandson? What's he been up to?' asked Basil.

Grindal looked him in the eye for the first time since they entered the house. His first thought was to make up some kind of story. His pride was already battered. But then he decided it was easier to tell the truth.

'A problem with drugs. I'm not really sure to be honest.' Grindal looked at him without blinking.

'Oh.' Basil nodded his head in affirmation and then averted his gaze.

'Please sit down and make yourselves comfortable. Kate is sound asleep; I don't think she'll wake up. If she does, tell her I'll be back soon . . . Would you like a cup of coffee? Or something to eat?' He pushed the television program into Basil's hand. Basil gave him a strange look. At that point Grindal realised he was not in full control. *Calm down, calm down, your acting like a complete dick head*. The thought caused him to re-focus. He took a deep breath.

'Anyway, just make yourselves comfortable. I'm sure you'll find whatever you need.' He spoke the words slowly. 'Oh shit, I haven't called a taxi yet,' he added more quickly.

Picking up the phone, he proceeded to dial for the taxi. Moira looked across at Basil and started to nod her head. Basil stared back at her dumbly, not knowing what she was trying to communicate.

'Don't worry about the taxi. Basil will take you in his car,' said Moira.

'I will?' The statement took him by surprise.

Grindal looked first at Moira and then at Basil.

'Are you sure?'

'Er . . . Yes. No, that's fine.'

There was no real enthusiasm in the offer, but Grindal was in a hurry. The urgency of the situation took precedence over his negative feelings towards Basil.

'Ok. Let's get going then.'

He picked up his coat that was slung over the back of a dining chair and headed for the door. Basil followed him out, hands in pockets, looking totally dejected.

'Footscray Police Station please,' said Grindal as they pulled away from the curbside.

Basil did not reply. The car was filled with a stony silence as he drove somewhat leisurely towards their destination.

'Nice car,' said Grindal, trying to ease the tension.

'Yes,' replied Basil. 'You don't drive, do you?' he added.

'I used to, but that was a few years ago. In any case I couldn't afford one. What with all the running costs and repairs. One like this must cost a bit to keep on the road?'

'Not really, they don't break down like they used to years ago,' replied Basil. 'Mind you, one of the main problems now is with vandals. Not so long ago I had all my tires let down right outside Moira's place. Would you believe it, all four?' he reiterated.

Grindal shook his head in mock disbelief.

'Some people have no respect for other people's property. Still I suppose it could have been worse. They might have slashed them.'

Basil gave Grindal a long sideways glance. 'If it happens again, I'll get the police involved.'

'Mmm.'

Grindal decided that the conversation might lead to somewhere he didn't want to go so he refrained from any further comment on the matter. The rest of the journey was completed in silence.

When they arrived at the Police Station Grindal made his way through the door and walked up to the counter. Basil had followed him in but stood back three or four paces from the front desk so that he could scrutinize the proceedings. There were no other members of the public inside the station. The uniformed officer behind the counter looked disdainfully at Grindal then at Basil.

'You two together?' he asked.

Grindal looked over his shoulder, he had not realised Basil had followed him.

'Yes.'

'What can I do for you sir?'

'I've come to pick up Josh Marshall,' Grindal said to the man on the desk.

The officer did not reply. Turning his back, he walked to the rear of the station where another uniformed man was sitting at a desk. After a short, mumbled conversation, the two officers returned to the counter. The second Officer had a large stomach which hung untidily over his belt. The bright red face was probably due to high blood pressure Grindal thought. The three stripes on his sleeve told Grindal who he was before he introduced himself.

'I'm Sargent Godwin. And you are?'

'Grindal Falcon. I'm the boy's Grandfather.'

'Do you have any identity sir?'

The Sargent leaned heavily on the counter staring Grindal in the face.

'Er . . . Yes, I should have something here somewhere.' He patted his pockets nervously looking for some kind of documentation that might identify him. Unfortunately, all he could find was an old bus ticket and his last bank statement which he had been searching for the day before without any luck. His wallet he had left back at the house. He cursed himself inwardly for not bringing it.

'I'm sorry but I don't seem to have my wallet with me.

All I have is this bank statement. It does have my name and address on it,' he added hopefully.

The Sargent took the statement from him and scrutinized it for some seconds.

'This is not really what I had in mind,' he said sarcastically. 'Don't you have a driver's license or something?'

Grindal was starting to get annoyed. He could imagine Basil's glee at his predicament. Nothing was going right. In his mind's eye, he saw himself leaning back over the counter and holding his face one inch from the Sargent's and saying,

'If I had a fucking driver's license then why would I be showing you a bank statement, you stupid fat prick.' He breathed deeply and made a real effort to control his surging emotions.

'Look I'm really sorry but that's all I have. Would you like me to go away and bring something else?'

The Sargent ignored Grindal and made a comment to his junior officer.

'I've got better things to do than waste my time with this lot. Wait here,' he said looking back at Grindal.

He then disappeared through a door at the rear of the station. Five minutes later he returned with Josh. Josh looked at Grindal and nodded. He had a bruise on his cheek and a small cut under his right eye.

'He's been charged with drinking underage and possession of an illegal substance. He's lucky he's not been charged with resisting arrest,' announced the Sargent.

'Are you all right Josh? They haven't been knocking you around have they?'

Grindal stared at the Sargent as he asked the question.

'No, I'm fine Grandad. Where's Mum?'

'I'll tell you in the car,' said Grindal.

'When you two have finished your little family chat, there is some paperwork to do,' interrupted the Sargent.

Grindal bit his lip. He knew that it was neither the time nor the place to let his temper get the better of him.

On the way home, Grindal sat in the back seat of the car with Josh. Initially it had been his intention to give him a lecture. He changed his mind. In the dim light of the car he saw the dejected look on Josh's face and realised the boy was nearly in tears. Instead, Grindal leaned back and closed his eyes. It had been a long day. He was tired and dejected. All he really wanted to do was sleep.

No one spoke until they were a full fifteen minutes into the journey home.

'Your mother was involved in a car accident today. She's in hospital,' said Grindal.

Josh lifted his head and turned quickly to face his Grandfather. His wide-open eyes were filled with alarm.

'Is she all right?'

She has a few broken bones and a bang on the head, but I'm sure she'll be fine. We'll go and visit her tomorrow,' he added quickly.

'What happened?'

Grindal related the details of the accident that were given to him by Mrs. Edwards. Josh sat silently, head bowed, staring blankly into his lap.

'I'm sorry about tonight,' he said eventually.

'Don't worry about it. We'll talk about it later,' said Grindal.

The rest of the journey was completed in silence.

As they walked into the house, Grindal turned to Basil and looked him in the eye.

'Thanks for the ride. I appreciate it.'

Basil nodded his head in response.

'No worries.'

****

CHAPTER 12

The following morning, they visited the hospital and were informed by the doctor that Clare would be there for at least four weeks. And even after that she would need constant care for quite some time. Four days passed before Clare could communicate properly with her family. Prior to that she had been slipping in and out of consciousness. At first Kate had been extremely distressed seeing her mother so badly bruised and unable to talk properly. But after Mum had given her a few assuring smiles she brightened up considerably.

Josh on the other hand was sullen and despondent. He was feeling guilty about the drug charge. He told his grandfather that he felt ashamed. He had let everyone down but didn't know what to do about it. Grindal was not sure how to handle the situation. There were so many other things to cope with all he could do was tell Josh not to worry, that things would work out.

Since the accident neither Josh nor Kate had been to school. They had spent most of the time at the hospital along with Grindal. There were no other visitors. Grindal had telephoned Gerry, Clare's friend from the Brotherhood and told him about the accident. Gerry was deeply concerned and said he would go to the hospital immediately. Grindal had insisted somewhat aggressively that no one could visit until he said so.

Clare was still in intensive care. Even though she appeared to be getting better each day, she was still a long way from full recovery. Josh, Kate and Grindal had been surviving on a diet of cereals, toasted sandwiches, beans on toast and take-aways. Neither Josh nor Grindal had any cooking skills. The single attempt Grindal made to cook something more palatable, had not even made the taste test. His beef patties he had watched Jessie prepare so many times had been rejected because they were visually sickening.

The fact that everyone was dejected did not help. Kate and Josh were withdrawn most of the time. Even though he had tried, Grindal was unable to motivate himself or his grandchildren. The house was in a mess. The laundry basket was full, and no one knew how to use an iron.

Seven days after the accident there was some good news. Clare had regained full consciousness and the doctors had decided that there was no apparent brain damage. When they went to the hospital that night, Clare greeted them with a big smile. Even though her face was still badly bruised, the sparkle had returned to her eyes. Explanations were not needed. They all knew she was going to get better. For Grindal, the relief was almost palpable. It was as if a large weight had been suddenly lifted from the inside of his being. He looked up to the ceiling and was almost tempted to thank the God he did not believe in.

The curtains around the bed were open. There were seven other beds in the ward, all were occupied, mostly by people recovering from major surgery. As was their custom, they walked quietly, not wishing to disturb the other patients.

'How are you feeling Mum?' asked Josh.

'Much better now I can stay awake for more than a couple of hours at a time,' replied Clare.

'Yes, I saw the doctor on the way in. He told me the good news,' said Grindal.

Kate sat carefully on the bed next to her mother. Clare attentively stroked the top of her head. 'Dear me Kate. How long since you brushed your hair? And look at your blouse. Looks as if it came straight out of the wash basket.'

'Yes, I'm afraid things have been a little hectic over the past few days, as you can well imagine,' interrupted Grindal. 'But now you're getting better I'm sure we'll be much more organized.'

'By the way, Gerry called earlier, he's been asking after you,' said Grindal, trying to change the subject.

'Yes, I know,' said Clare with a frown. 'He sent me a card and two letters. I only got to read them today. He tells me you prevented him or any of the group from visiting.'

'I'm sorry, I just thought that....'

'Don't worry Dad, you're probably right. I haven't really been up to seeing anyone. Apart from that, I must look a real mess. They're moving me to the general ward tomorrow. Doctor said I should be on my feet in no time. I certainly hope so. I'm sick of using a bedpan . . . Anyway, how have you all been coping?'

'Not as well as when you're around Mum,' said Josh.

'I hope you're all eating properly,' said Clare. What did you have for tea tonight?'

'We had fish and chips from the fish and chip shop,' said Kate. 'There not as good as you make them, but they're much better than grandad's meat patties.'

'I didn't know you could make meat patties Dad?'

Grindal just shrugged his shoulders.

As usual they caught the bus home from the hospital. It was dark outside. In the dim light, Grindal looked at his grandchildren as they sat together in the seat opposite. They were much happier in the knowledge that their mother was going to be alright. The comment Clare had made about Kate's hair and blouse made Grindal realise that he was not doing too well organizing the home front. The truth was, Kate and Josh looked like a pair of street urchins and he didn't look much better.

Not good enough Falcon, you useless bastard. It's not fair on the kids or Clare. From now on things are going to change. With that thought in mind, he resolved that from the next day onwards he would take charge of the situation. He would start solving problems instead of complaining about them.

When they arrived home, Kate and Josh slumped into the sofa and turned on the television. Normally Grindal would join them but instead he went into the kitchen and made all three of them a mug of Ovaltine. He set the drinks on the table and called out to his grandchildren.

'Josh, Kate, turn off the television and come into the kitchen. Special family meeting.' Neither of them moved. 'Come on, chop chop.' He banged the table with the flat of his hand.

They were not used to their grandfather shouting at them, never mind banging on the table. Thinking it must be something serious, Josh and Kate went quickly into the kitchen. The three of them sat facing each other.

'What's the matter grandad?' asked Kate.

'Nothings the matter Kate. At least nothing we can't fix

if we all work together.'

'What do you mean?' said Josh.

'Well, while we were coming home on the bus, I got to thinking what your mother had said about Kate. How her blouse was crumpled, and her hair was not brushed properly. And she was right. Look at us, we look like three hobos.'

'What's a hobo grandad?' asked Kate.

'Someone who doesn't care how they look. Someone who lives rough with no proper home.'

Josh looked down at himself then at Grindal and his sister. 'I suppose you're right.'

'Well, the thing is, your mother sees us like this and even though she doesn't say anything, I'm sure she's worried to death. Wondering how we're coping without her here. Now is that true or not?'

Josh nodded his head. 'But what can we do about it?'

'From tomorrow on we're going to work as a team. I'll do most of the work, but I need your help. We're going to clean the house, wash the clothes, and even get the ironing done one way or another. And another thing, from now on there'll be no more take-away's ... Well, at least not as many. I'm going to make us something decent for dinner tomorrow, even if it takes me all day.'

'Starting tomorrow, you two go back to school. Mum's

going to be ok now, so the sooner things get back to normal, the better it will be for all of us.'

'Oh, not school,' Josh growled.

'Yes school. We'll get up early and I'll work out which bus I can catch with Kate. Josh, you can go on your bike as usual. I rang the school last week to say you wouldn't be in. Maybe I should write a note for you both to give to your teachers.'

'On second thoughts, Josh you write your teachers name on a piece of paper for me before you go to bed. I'll speak to Kate's teacher personally.' Grindal didn't wait for any more comment. 'Now, into the shower and off to bed with you both. Grandad's going to iron some cloths for us to wear tomorrow.'

Three hours later Grindal crawled into bed. He was exhausted. It had taken forever to iron the cloths they were to wear the next day. Following his discovery that the iron melted the designs on the front of the tee shirts things went a little better. That was, after he spent half an hour scraping the melted plastic from the bottom of the iron. Even then, close scrutiny would reveal lots of creases in the wrong places. After that he had packed lunches and written the note to Josh's teacher. Even though he was worn out, Grindal was pleased with himself and even more determined to bring everything back to normal before Clare was released from the hospital.

One thing he was not so sure about was Josh's problem. His trial was coming up the following week. He couldn't decide whether to tell Clare. He didn't want to give her the worry. But imagine if Josh got put away for a few weeks. What would he tell her then? It was his hope that it would just be a fine and he would tell Clare when it was all settled. That would be the most convenient conclusion to the episode. But Grindal knew from experience, the word convenient was not the one which normally came to mind at the conclusion of past problems.

Josh had been reluctant to talk about the episode with Grindal. He insisted that it was just a minor offence that would result in a fine. Grindal was not so sure. He decided he would discuss the problem with Garth. He knew about the law and pot and stuff like that. He would know what to do.

The following day after he had taken Kate to school Grindal called into the Benders'. Garth greeted him at the door.

'Ah Falcon. I was wondering where you'd got to. We haven't seen you for a couple of weeks. I thought you'd left the country or been put in jail or something. Come in, come in.'

As was the usual ritual when he called in, the coffee was brewed immediately, and he, Garth and Tulip, sat at the kitchen table discussing the latest events. Grindal told them in detail what had happened over the past couple of weeks. Although they had never met Clare, they were genuinely concerned about her situation and greatly relieved when Grindal informed them that she was now recovering.

'So how are you coping?' asked Tulip.

'Not too badly,' replied Grindal. I made an executive decision that we would straighten things up in the house and try and bring some order back into everyone's life. I really let things go over these past few days. The house is in a mess. Dirty washing, un-ironed clothes.'

'I did a crash course in ironing last night. Most of the stuff I did looked better before I started. Look at this.' Grindal laughed and held up his arms pointing to the semi-crumpled shirt he was wearing.

'You silly man. Why on earth didn't you let us know you were in trouble.' From now on, you bring the ironing over here,' said Tulip. 'What about the washing?'

'Oh, the washing's a snack. All you do is throw everything in the machine, add some soap powder, not too much mind, then let it rip.'

'Sounds as if you're a real expert at the washing

Falcon,' said Garth.

'Too right,' agreed Grindal.

'Anyway, I insist you bring the ironing over,' said Tulip.

'Well maybe just the kid's stuff. A bit embarrassing for them to go to school with crumpled clothes. I don't really care about me,' said Grindal.

'What about food. Are you eating properly?' asked Tulip.

'Oh no worries about that. I'm a dab hand at cooking,' lied Grindal.

'I didn't know that,' said Garth. 'Maybe you can come over here one night and cook us one of your specialties?'

Grindal looked at him but did not reply. The topic of food reminded him he had to prepare something for dinner that night.

'Actually, my main problem is Josh,' said Grindal slowly.

'Really, what's he been up to then? Not getting underage girls pregnant or anything like that?' said Garth, smiling.

'No, nothing like that. Could be more serious, depending which way you look at it,' replied Grindal. He paused for a few seconds to gather his thoughts.

'He was picked up the other week for possessing drugs.'

Garth looked surprised. 'Not the hard stuff I hope?'

'No, thankfully. From what I can gather it was a small amount of marihuana. Trouble is he won't really talk about it. He seems to think it's no big deal. He reckons he doesn't even need a solicitor. I don't really know what to do. I remembered that you had a certificate on your study wall that said you were a Bachelor of Law, so I thought you'd be just the right person to ask.'

He smiled rather sheepishly and for some reason he could not understand, Grindal felt a sudden rush of embarrassment.

Garth tapped the table with his fingers and pursed his lips thoughtfully.

'Send him around here when he gets home from school. From what you've told me I think it might be advisable if we had a little chat.'

'I don't know if he'll come. I can't make him,' said Grindal.

'Just tell him that I smoke dope too, so I should know what I'm talking about.'

'Thanks for that Garth. I really appreciate it.'

'Think nothing of it Falcon. Besides I haven't done

anything yet.'

When Grindal left the Benders', he was feeling much better. On reflection, he decided that it was good to have friends to share your problems with. This thought was reinforced as he arrived home. He checked the mail. There was just one letter. It was addressed to him. Just as he was about to enter the front door, he heard a female voice calling him from next door.

'Hello.'

It was Moira, and if Grindal guessed correctly, she was carrying a very large casserole dish.

'Hello Moira. How are you today?' Grindal smiled in anticipation.

'Good thank you. I thought you might like to try some of this casserole?' She looked embarrassed as she proffered the dish towards him. 'I hope you don't think I'm intruding,' she added.

'No certainly not,' said Grindal. 'I'd love to try your casserole, we all would.' He relieved her of the dish. It was still warm and gave off a beefy aroma that made his mouth water.

'Thanks very much.'

'How's Clare, I do hope she's feeling better?'

'Yes, she's much better thanks. Hopefully she'll be

coming home in another week or so.'

'That is good news. I bet Josh and Kate are really missing her.'

'That's for sure,' replied Grindal.

'How are you coping anyway? I've been meaning to ask if you need any help, but I didn't want you to think I was intruding.'

'No don't worry about that. If you call this intruding,' said Grindal holding up the casserole dish. 'Then the more you do it, the better we'll all feel. I don't mind admitting Moira; I'm not really much use when it comes to the culinary arts. And we're all getting sick of Pizza.'

He smiled at her begging the answer to the unasked question.

'Well why on earth didn't you say something? You know how I love to cook. I'll tell you what, just leave it with me and I'll see what I can cook up for you all, at least a couple of nights a week anyway.'

'That would be wonderful. Thank you very much... Better get this in the oven,' said Grindal, excusing himself from the conversation.

'Oh, and how's Basil?' he asked as an afterthought.

'He's fine, really proud of himself. He won the bowling club singles championship on the weekend.' Moira smiled enthusiastically.

'My my, he just has so much talent.' Grindal closed the front door. 'Fucking prick.'

He took the casserole to the kitchen and placed it straight into the oven. *With a few boiled spuds and some frozen peas, it'll be a meal fit for a king.*

He took the letter from his pocket and looked at it thoughtfully. There was no window on it, so it wasn't a bill. He ripped it open and read the contents.

Dear Mr. Falcon,

We are pleased to advise that an offer of $22,000 has been made for your property situated at 47 Harris Street Newport West. Please contact the undersigned as soon as possible should you wish to proceed with the matter.

Yours faithfully,

D. Conan

Cromwell Real Estate Agents

Grindal rubbed his eyes and re- read the part that said twenty-two thousand. 'Dam right I wish to proceed with the matter'. He shook his head in amazement. When he had signed up with the Cromwell's' he remembered they had discussed a lot of money, but he had not really believed it. After all, he and Jessie had bought the land for a few hundred pounds.

'Twenty-two thousand, Jesus fucking Christ, I'm rich.'

******

CHAPTER 13

It was a clear sunny day, the first day of spring in fact. It had been almost three months since he had received his letter from Cromwell's. The money was now in the bank, at least most of it was.

Standing at the gate Grindal cast his gaze across the house and garden. The damaged leaking gutter had been replaced and repainted along with the rest of the house. The cracked concrete that had once been the footpath had been dug up and, in its place, there was now a neat walkway of pavers. Flowers Clare had planted only a few weeks ago were already bursting their buds and promised a multi-coloured display to contrast the new timber palings bordering the front garden.

He reflected for a moment. Life was good. The last three months had been a magical time. Everything he had worried about had not happened. Everything he had hoped for had come to pass.

Clare was well and getting stronger every day. Josh was not in jail; he was back at school and working hard. Grindal was not sure what had passed between Josh and Garth Bender, but Garth had really made an impression on him. He had found him a solicitor and even went to court to speak on Josh's behalf. At the end of the day he was fined sixty-five dollars, with no conviction recorded. Garth told Grindal that the solicitor was an old friend and did the case for free, Grindal was not so sure. At any rate, it was a top outcome. He had even managed to keep it from Clare. Josh, Kate and Grindal had agreed that it would be their secret.

Two weeks previous, Grindal had decided that a celebration was in order. He had reasoned with Clare that it would good to bring a few people together who had helped both him and the family over the past weeks. As the idea gathered momentum it was decided that a joint birthday party would be in order. Clare and Grindal had birthdays only three days apart and since neither could remember the last time they had a birthday party, everyone agreed it was a good idea. Grindal insisted he would pay for caterers to do all the work. Clare had protested strongly about this but relented when the rest of the family took Grindal's side.

******

The new garden gate opened noiselessly, Grindal worked it a few times then nodded his head with satisfaction. He looked at his watch, it was six thirty, just time enough to get something to eat before the caterers arrived.

There was an air of excitement in the house. Clare had cleaned and vacuumed every room. Bruce their dog was boarding overnight with the local Vet. With nothing else to do, she sat nervously waiting for the caterers to arrive. Josh and Kate were arguing over which music should be played at what time. The birthday party was a new experience for them all. Because the house was small, they had decided on using both inside and outside areas. The caterers would set up a barbecue outside where they would cook steak, chops and sausages. The salads and cakes would be laid out on the dining room table. Grindal had taken it upon himself to organize the drinks. Clare had not been very impressed when she saw the amount of alcohol he had brought into the house. He had eventually pacified her with assurances that everyone he had invited was responsible and definitely not prone to heavy drinking. At least that's what he hoped.

The thought had occurred to him that perhaps Clare's guests might not appreciate the company of homosexuals and dope smokers. But he had reasoned they were all nice enough people, after a few drinks it wouldn't matter. Luckily, alcohol was not on the banned list for members of The Brotherhood of the Second Coming.

Activities in the Brotherhood had gone a bit quiet

lately. With no one really wanting to take up the leadership role after the mysterious swift exit of Brother James, there was talk of disbanding the group. The last meeting held at the house had been a very lack luster affair. Grindal had almost fallen asleep. Still he had done his bit for the group, even if they didn't know about it.

A loud knock on the front door announced the arrival of the caterers. Moira had recommended Dino's Mobile Catering Service to Grindal, assuring him of their professionalism, cleanliness and affordability. Grindal had deduced from that statement that they provided good food at the right price. He opened the door.

'Good afternoon, my name is Dino and these two ladies are my assistants.'

Dino had thick bushy grey hair with matching eyebrows. The woman wore black skirts and white blouses. Dino looked very smart in black trousers and white shirt, but Grindal thought the bow tie was a bit of overkill.

In single file, the three caterers walked straight passed Grindal and into the lounge room, where Clare waited in anticipation.

'Good afternoon madam, you must be the lady of the house. My name is Dino. This is my wife Marika and my daughter Angelina.'

Marika smiled but Angelina looked as if she would rather be somewhere else.

'With your permission, I will look around your very nice house and then we will prepare the food.'

'Yes certainly,' said Clare. 'Is there anything I can get you?'

'No, no, you just relax. Dino will arrange everything'.

'We thought we would put the salads and stuff in here and do the meat outside,' interrupted Grindal.

'Yes Mr. Filcan, I can see that.' Dino gave Grindal a contemptuous glare.

After a quick look around, he started giving orders to his two assistants who quickly responded bringing in lots of boxes, trays and bags from the small-refrigerated van that was parked in the street. Dino busied himself trundling a very large mobile barbecue to the back of the house. In the meantime, Grindal had decided to stay right out of the catering and busied himself organizing the drinks. Within an hour they were ready. Dino and his able assistants were sipping on a cup of their own coffee, waiting for the guests to appear. The timing was perfect.

Garth and Tulip Bender were the first to arrive. Garth was carrying a bottle of wine and Tulip held a small posy of flowers.

'Come in, come in,' said Grindal leading Tulip by the hand. 'Let me introduce you to Clare.'

He made the introductions. Garth acknowledged Clare with a nod of his head and a smile. The two women shook hands.

'Hope your feeling much better now?' said Tulip. 'I brought you some flowers.'

'Oh, they're gorgeous. Thank you. Dad's told me so much about you and Garth. I can't thank you enough for helping out with things when I was in hospital.'

'No, it was nothing, I should have realised sooner that men are not much good with household chores. Still it's a good job your dad's such a good cook, otherwise there might have been some real problems.'

'Who Dad, a good cook?'

'Ah let me get you a drink Tulip,' interrupted Grindal. 'Chardonnay, isn't it?'

'Yes, thanks, that will be fine.'

Kate then joined her mother and the conversation changed to another subject.

'What do you want Garth, beer, wine, scotch?'

As he led Garth towards the icebox containing the drinks, Grindal leaned over and spoke quietly. 'You won't smoke any of that hooch of yours in the house, will you?'

'Never worry Falcon, you know me, the height of discretion.'

'And especially don't let Josh have any,' said Grindal ignoring the assurance.

'His mother would have a heart attack.'

The knocks on the door were now coming more frequently. Gerry had arrived and was fussing around Clare almost to the point of embarrassment. There was quite a few the Brotherhood invited. Although Grindal knew most, he had nothing much in common with them. A nod of his head and a smile was his usual method of communication. He was surprised to see one or two helping themselves to large glasses of scotch and wondered what that might lead to later in the night.

There was a sudden turning of heads followed by a discernable hush in the conversation. Grindal was at the far end of the kitchen and had to stand on his toes to see what was happening.

'Hello everyone.'

An opening appeared as people stepped back.

There, resplendent in bright red suit with matching cowboy hat and feather, was Damien holding a large bouquet of flowers. Roy was standing directly behind him looking somewhat embarrassed.

Hurrying through the room Grindal went to greet them. He had neglected to tell his daughter that there were two poofters on the guest list. The main reason being that they were on the banned list as far as the Brotherhood was concerned. Although, considering the tastes of recent leadership he couldn't think why.

'Hello Roy, Damien. You found your way here alright?'

'Yes, not a problem.'

Damien grabbed Grindal in a bear hug and gave him a kiss on the cheek. He felt his cheeks flush with embarrassment. From the corner of his eye he saw Gerry and Clare staring with mouths wide open.

Oh, what the fuck, he returned the hug with equal enthusiasm. Roy finally came to the rescue pulling Grindal to one side.

'Why don't you introduce us to your family?' He smiled. 'Don't worry, the flowers are for your daughter.'

'Ah, Clare, Gerry, I'd like to introduce you to my friends Roy and Damien. Remember I told you about Roy. He's the one who pulled me out of the fire.'

Roy shook hands with Clare and Gerry, who were still stunned by the sight of someone wearing a red suit and a cowboy hat. Damien gave a flourishing bow and presented the large bouquet.

'For you Madame.'

Clare took the flowers. 'Thank you, I'll er… put them in a vase. Would you excuse me a minute?'

She hurried off not knowing what else to say. Damien sidled up to Gerry. 'Nice place you have here. Been here long?'

'No, only about half an hour.' He glanced quickly from side to side looking for an escape route.

Damien posed in front of Gerry commanding his attention. 'How do you like the threads, not bad eh?'

'Yes, very colorful. Er … would you excuse me a minute, I need to go to the toilet.'

With that he hurried off, glancing back over his shoulder to make sure he was not being followed.

Roy and Grindal had watched the confrontation with some amusement.

'You're not trying to put the hard word on my future son in law, are you? Come on I'll get you a drink.'

They wandered into the kitchen where Garth and Tulip stood sipping their wine. After a brief introduction Grindal left the four of them chatting merrily.

It was getting warm inside the house so Grindal decided to go outside for some fresh air. As he was standing by the front gate a noisy old Ford pulled up in front of the house. He looked closely wondering who it might be. He didn't have to wait long.

'G'day Grindal, how the fuck are you?'

He immediately recognised the face of the man who jumped out of the passenger seat of the car, it was Taff.

'Well I'll be dammed; I see you got my invitation then?'

The two men shook hands vigorously.

'When I rang up whoever answered the phone said you were away for a few weeks, but I sent the invitation anyway. Good to see you Taff.'

'Yeah, I came back early. I've been doing a few stints in the bush lately… Pain in the arse, but the money's good.'

Grindal looked at the back of the man who was trying unsuccessfully to lock the car door. The shape looked vaguely familiar.

'Who did you bring with you Taff?'

The man turned and walked towards them.

'Oh, for fuck's sake, why did you bring him?'

The stumpy unkempt figure of Sid Boucher lurched towards them.

'Well he offered to give me a lift and I didn't think you'd mind.'

'Mind…. Look at him dressed like a bag of shit and hasn't even combed his hair. For fuck's sake.'

'Well I can't really tell him to go away now, can I?'

'Alright…. Alright.' Grindal was annoyed. Boucher was one of the last people on earth he would invite to his house.

'G'day Grindal. Nice to see you again.'

Boucher offered his hand. Grindal ignored it.

'Listen, you can come in and have a drink, but stay out of the way. Don't annoy any of the women, or the men. Don't pick your nose or play with your dick. Understand?'

'Yeah no worries.'

Boucher smiled and sidled up to the house as if he had just received a warm welcome.

'For fuck's sake Grindal repeated shaking his head. 'Come on let's have a drink and you can fill me in on what's been happening at the dragon's den in Moonee Ponds.'

The two men followed Boucher, who had already let himself in through the front door. Grindal was not surprised when all eyes turned on Boucher. Probably thinking he was some kind of gatecrasher. He took him by the arm and led him to the kitchen, shoved a cold bottle of beer into his hand.

'Don't move.'

Clare had followed them into the kitchen and was still

eyeing Boucher suspiciously. Taking her by the arm Grindal led her away.

'Don't worry about him, he's just a homeless derro that Taff here has been trying to help out.'

He gave Taff an appropriate dig in the side to make sure he had got the message.

'You haven't met Taff have you? He's one of the people that lived in the boarding house.'

Clare shook hands.

'From what Dad's been telling me, it's a wonder anyone at all lives there?'

'Yes, I wonder myself at times, but I never seem to get around to moving out.'

Clare looked over at Boucher who was scratching his balls with one hand and holding his beer in the other.

'Your friend over there, have you known him very long?'

Taff ignored the question.

'Bit of a sad case really; I think he came from a dysfunctional family. Still, he's quite harmless.'

Clare shook her head and went back into the sitting room.

Grindal appointed Josh to keep a close eye on him.

With drinks in hand, the two men wandered

outside. Dino was in the process of lighting the barbecue. He gave them a nod and an imitation smile.

'Everything alright?' asked Grindal.

'Everything is fine, Mr. Filcan.'

They slowly wandered over to a wooden bench that was placed strategically on the edge of the new landscaped back lawn.

'So, tell me Taff, what's been happening at your place since I left? Are you and Paddy still at it?'

Taff smiled. 'Paddy's in jail.'

'What for?'

'Assault and battery. Assault with intent to do bodily harm and fuck knows what else.'

'Who copped that from him?'

Taff rubbed his forefinger along the edge of his nose. It was then that Grindal noticed the slight hook that had not been there before.

'What, you?'

'Irish prick. Caught me letting his tires down. Kicked shit out of me he did. I was in hospital for a week.'

'You silly bastard,' said Grindal. 'He was bound to catch you one day. Lucky he didn't kill you.'

Taff laughed. 'Yeah, that's what the judge said... Anyway, fuck him. He'll be inside for at least another six months… I suppose I'll have to find somewhere else to live. The bastard threatened to kill me when he gets out. I was thinking I might go interstate.'

'Sounds like a good idea to me,' said Grindal.

What about the dragon Fromp what's she up to?'

'Calmed down a lot lately. Really mellowed in fact. What with her new grandson to look after, she's gone really clucky.'

'And the Ferret?'

'Disappeared from the face of the earth. No one's heard from him since he left hospital.'

'Come on, let's get another drink and see what that prick Boucher is up to.'

After standing in the kitchen on his own for twenty minutes, Boucher started to fidget, rubbing his stomach. 'I need to shit,' he mumbled to himself. A few seconds later he walked down the passageway to look for the only toilet in the house. When he found it, Mrs. Walters, an older member of The Brotherhood was waiting in line. She looked at Boucher for a few seconds then patted him on the back.

'You must be that poor homeless man that Grindal mentioned?'

Boucher stared at her without responding.

'I can solve all of your problems,' said a now animated

Mrs. Walters.

Boucher continued to stare.

'Let me bring you to Jesus, he'll find a way. Soon you will cast away all of your sorrows. You will become a new person.'

Mrs. Walters opened her arms wide.

'Come to Jesus.'

'What the fuck....' Boucher turned and almost ran out of the front door in his bid to escape.

It was quiet outside. He looked around, there was a big bush by the side of the fence. 'Perfect,' he said to himself. He positioned himself at the back of the bush, threw off the top half of his overhauls, dropped his underpants and proceeded to evacuate his bowels. When he had finished, he realised that the bush did not come with a roll of toilet paper. 'Oh Well,' he shrugged. He pulled on his overhauls and let out a long sigh. 'That's much better.'

Unfortunately, instead of leaving his droppings on the lawn behind the bush, they were now sitting in the back of his overhauls. In his haste, he had omitted make sure his clothing was clear of the drop zone.

The loud refrain of Chubby Checker singing "Let's Twist Again" was coming from inside. 'Ooh my favourite,' said Boucher, as he hurried back into the house.

As he entered the house, Grindal took in the scene before him. Damien was in the middle of the room with Moira, dancing at full throttle. They were doing their impromptu version of "The Twist." The rest of the guests were watching on and clapping.

Suddenly there was a new dancer on the floor. A disheveled looking Boucher joined the two performers and started to give his own version of the dance. Everyone howled with laughter as he wriggled and swayed around the floor totally out of sync with the music. He stood on one leg and wiggled the other one in the air.

Abruptly, the laughter stopped. A large turd, which would have made Bruce the dog jealous, had fallen from the wriggling leg of Boucher's crumpled overhauls.

'Oh no, he's shit himself,' said Grindal out loud.

Everyone in the room, including Boucher was staring in disbelief at the large brown dropping on the sitting room floor.

'Taff, get him out of here,' shouted Grindal.

Taff responded with lighting speed and removed Boucher from the room, consigning him to plastic chair at the back of the yard. Tulip Bender swiftly transferred the turd onto a disposable plate before unceremoniously dumping it into the toilet.

The room was quiet, everyone was staring at the floor which was now being cleaned and disinfected by Clare. The silence was unexpectedly broken by a muffled snigger which came from the back of the room. It seemed to be infectious. Within seconds, there were more. Soon the whole room was filled with raucous laughter. It seemed that everyone in the room could see the comical side of what had just occurred.

Grindal was relieved, and even had a chuckle himself.

'What are you smiling at, you old maggot?' said Garth.

He looked across at Garth and laughed. He'd heard the expression before but was dammed if he could remember when.

END

About the Author

G'day, my name is Tony Wallis author of 'Adventures of an Old Maggot'. I live in South Australia, where I spent most of my working life in the construction industry. The colourful characters I met, the situations I encountered and the places I lived in over the years, were the basis for the novel.

I have been writing for many years and have an Advanced Diploma in Professional Writing, however, for the most part this has been technical and commercial in content. 'Adventures of an Old Maggot' is my first novel and I am currently writing a follow up which I hope to have completed in the coming months.

If you enjoyed the story, this 'Old Maggot' would very much appreciate it if you could write a short review on Amazon, (or anywhere else that might be appropriate). If you have any comments or questions, please visit my blog at www.boomereview.com you may even enjoy some of the posts I have written over the past couple of years.

I Hope to bring you some more adventures of a different type very soon.

Thanks for your support,

Tony Wallis